DOWNERS GROVE

ALSO BY MICHAEL HORNBURG

Bongwater

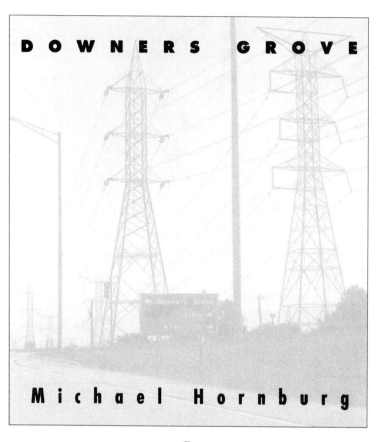

DOWNERS GROVE

Michael Hornburg

GROVE PRESS / NEW YORK

First published in 1999 by William Morrow and Company, Inc., New York

Published simultaneously in Canada
Printed in the United States of America

FIRST GROVE PRESS EDITION

Library of Congress Cataloging-in-Publication Data

Hornburg, Michael.
    Downers Grove / Michael Hornburg.
        p.   cm.
    ISBN 0-8021-3793-8
    1. High school students—Fiction. 2. Teenage girls—Fiction. 3. Illinois—Fiction.
I. Title.

PS3558.O6873 D69 2001
813'.54—dc21   00-066345

Grove Press
841 Broadway
New York, NY 10003

01 02 03 04   10 9 8 7 6 5 4 3 2 1

This one's for Abbie Jones

D O W N E R S   G R O V E

LYING in the yard tearing out clumps of grass, watching a jet draw a white line across the sky, I wanted to have a vision or some major introspection, to feel possessed and hallucinatory, to know, if only for a moment, that God really existed. Fluffy white clouds towered into the heavens like one dream piled on top of the next; a whole sky of afterthoughts polluting the air. The faces of movie stars, the shapes of dead pets, all lurked within the shifting vapor. Pressing my fingers between the blades of grass I focused on the gravity sucking me to the surface, imagined the slow rotation of the earth, its massive size, its ambient orbit, the endless void of the universe, but curiosity only seemed to accelerate my potential for a psychotic break.

My name is Crystal Methedrine Swanson, but my friends call me Chrissie. The name was part of some bad joke my parents formed in the confusion of my birth. Dad signed off on the name while Mom was in a narcotic dreamsleep, totally wiped out after fifteen hours of labor. He says I was conceived during a crystal meth excursion in the north woods of Wisconsin, hence the name. Mom says Dad is an idiot.

I'm seventeen years old, it's summertime, and there's an underlying sense of anticipation churning through my nervous system, as if a meteorite were screaming toward me this very second from the black depths of outer space. Which is good, 'cause I'm definitely in need of a change. I've outgrown my pink and white gingham bathing suit. The white lace trim is worn and frayed. It makes me feel like an oversize Lolita without anyone to seduce. Parked on a blanket, burning calories reading dirty books loaned from my mother's library, sometimes I feel like the sun is my only voyeur.

School sucked today. All the usual shit, senior year 60516. Sitting in my algebra class, listening to the formulas, the calculations, the answers, the endless steps that needed to be memorized, I started vegging out and began to imagine myself crumbling into dust and falling onto the floor. I had a scary thought that nobody would even notice, and then, in the middle of the night I'd be swept away in the rustling bristles of the janitor's broom.

I looked around the classroom, tried to imagine everyone twenty years from now: Who was the housewife? Who was in jail? Who was the car accident?

Maybe I should dye my hair purple? Maybe I should try to be more social? Maybe I should stop talking to myself? It's Friday afternoon and there's a thousand voices telling me what's wrong, examining the problems, making up new ones. Suburbs are the ghettos of meaninglessness.

M O M

MOM came home from work and dragged my brother and me to a Parents without Partners potluck. I protested most of the way there, but it was potluck or starve. Anyway, that's how Mom put it. This tall swarthy astronaut type named Dan has been hitting on Mom for the past month, and tonight we get to meet the swaggering bachelor under the shadow of the Ten Commandments.

"Best behavior," she warned, then clicked on the turn signal, took a deep breath, stared longingly at the church—kind of weary, kind of sad—and veered into the gravel parking lot of Saint John's Lutheran Church, a squat white-stone building off Route 53 in Lisle.

Started on the fly in the seventies, the place was obviously rolling in the dough by now. Part fallout bunker, part shrine to blandness, the building reeked of ammonia. We piled out of the car, locked the doors. Mom straightened her jacket, swept David's hair away from his eyes.

For all it's worth, churches seem like just another stop on the consumer highway, the crucifix a groovy logo for mystical life insurance. It really shows how desperate people are to have acceptable delusions of paranormal experience, of life after death in a world full of angels far beyond the clouds.

Mom forked over the tickets and made small talk with the church ladies. My brother and I hung up our coats, admiring the trophy case beside the church office. The cinder-block hallways smelled of the afterburn of sports: dried sweat and dirty sneakers. There were hot dogs and sloppy joes brewing in the gymnasium, potato salad stacked high, four different Jell-Os, and deviled eggs from here to Naperville. A massive crucifix hung above the electronic scoreboard. Red and white felt banners claimed conference championships 1992 and 1995. The room echoed with chatter. Mom looked at me sorta worried, and I smiled back all virginal and sweet, but we were as obvious as a hair ball on a white carpet. The astronaut spotted us before we made it to the food line. My brother, looking his usual morbid self, slouched into a folding chair and drifted toward an interlude with another dimension, totally insensitive to Mom's freaking.

When she introduced us, the astronaut shook my hand really hard like some two-bit candidate running for office, when I know all he had on his filthy mind was the cheap hot tub hotel on Ogden Avenue or wherever the hell it is these two trade laundry. He blushed, looking as happy as a game show contestant. I could tell right away that Mom was attracted to his confidence and stability. The astronaut was as far away from

Dad as Jell-O is to mashed potatoes. She liked it that he be-
longed to a church and that this was our first peek into the
sunshine of his mysterious galaxy.

A long line of wide bodies was hunched over the smorgas-
board. I picked up a white paper plate and plastic fork, then
took a place at the end of the line. Supper was a showcase of
sloppy joes, baked beans, and various mayonnaise salads brimming from the edges of clear plastic Tupperware bowls. I did
the best I could.

DANDELION

MOM got kind of defensive on the way home, insisted Dan was cute, that he had potential. I gave him the finger-down-the-throat award.

"I'm sorry no guys my age wear Doc Martens." She switched on the car radio and turned it up loud, as if she didn't want to hear what I had to say.

"I hope you're not thinking of doing anything irrational," I said.

Mom got all silent and weird, and I worried about her, saw her aging in front of me, all alone in that big house, drunk with her habits—straightening the silverware drawer, bundling up old newspapers for recycling. The radio crackled under the power lines and the song disappeared, then the radio crackled again and the song popped back. Mom turned it up, sang along to bits and pieces of the chorus.

"Some songs get stuck in my head forever," she said. "I must've heard this one a million times by now."

"Makes you realize brainwashing is for real," I said.

"You kids are so cynical. As soon as you smell sentimentality an alarm goes off." She twirled her hand around like a siren-light. "You have no respect for the past," she said, then sang along again, her head swaying back and forth in that half-crazy way that meant *trouble*. Whenever Dad didn't show up or things didn't go as planned Mom picked up a happy-go-lucky sway and shook it shoulder to shoulder like all she wanted to do for the rest of her life was dance.

"It's all that television, all that MTV, you think you're so modern." She shifted from third gear down to second rolling up to a stop sign. "And those computers. The Internet. All of a sudden the world is flush with typists. You'll all grow up to be secretaries." She laughed.

"David would look good in a dress," I said.

"Shut up," he said.

"You shut up," I said.

Mom smirked as if she had won.

Every time we roll down Maple Avenue and pass the watertower I get a wicked case of cotton mouth. It glows blue-green at night, sorta eerie, like some alien sci-fi space station. I always wondered why people would want to live on a barren planet and call it an adventure. It's bad enough growing up in a dead-end town like Downers Grove, but at least there's a drive-thru when you're thirsty. And someday I'll have my own apartment with a refrigerator full of ice cream and beer and I'll paint the walls all purple and gold like some bodacious Egyptian queen. There'll be lots of oversize white lace pillows, and organic grapes, and beeswax candles, and hardbody slaves, like that cute mechanic who works over at the gas station on Sixty-third and Main.

But then, bouncing over the Burlington Northern tracks, it dawned on me that Mom probably had the same kind of fantasies when she was my age, and now she was a lonely cowgirl with two teenagers stuffed into her holster and that I was a younger, trashier version of her. I tried to keep it all to myself, but then looked around and realized that in the general scope of things, everyone in the car was fucked.

Mom turned into our subdivision. The split-level houses were identical to one another in shape, the only significant trademarks were the exterior choices of paint or stain. A couple of pioneers had water sprinklers swishing over their yellowing sod. Our next-door neighbor was having his lawn sprayed by some top gun exterminator boy in a crisp white ChemLawn uniform. Dr. Jewels was in the driveway telling junior where to squirt that big black hose. Jewels is a nickname, his real name is Woskanovitz or something like that. We call him Jewels because he wears more jewelry then Zsa Zsa Gabor. Rings, bracelets, medallions, even the hubcaps of his Cadillac are gold. The man buys jewelry for his car.

As we pulled into the driveway I heard Mom gurgle a wet sigh. She looked sad. When I got out of the car to open the garage door I noticed a yellow dandelion had pushed its way through the rocks outlining our driveway, so I stomped on it with my boot.

"Why'dya do that for?" the lithium candidate asked while struggling out of the car. He leaned down all sensitive and stupid, cupping the flower in his hand, trying to fix it, set it up straight or something, but that sucker was already dead as yes-terday. Jewels payed big bucks to kill dandelions while Mom clipped the leaves and mixed them in her salads. Maybe that's what separates Republicans from Democrats.

I went upstairs, curled on my bed, and tried to figure out why I am who I am and what I need to do to mend the situ-ation. It's a charming form of psychic mutilation I slink into whenever I'm depressed. I wish I knew how to play guitar. Why is everything so hard?

A few minutes later there was a timid knock at my door. Mom flippped on the light and sat on the edge of my bed, looking guilty, then apologized for dragging us to the Brady Bunch clinic. I said it's okay, that I know she's lonely, and so she kissed my forehead, but still looked all freaked out. I wor-ried that Mom's insecurities were clashing with my own, that her life seemed as unpredictable as mine, but there wasn't much I could do. She stood, turned off the light, and closed the door. I moshed my face against the pillow and tried to dredge up some fantasy that would lure me into drowsiness but couldn't concentrate, because I'm worried about Mom, about us, and about everything.

D A D

JUST for the record, Dad was as universal as a stop sign. He was a musician-slash-mailman, a government job handed to him on a silver platter after his tour of Vietnam. He was a gambler, a poker player, a man who knew how to win with lousy cards. He always bragged it was a game of skill, not of chance. There were a few dusty trophies over the washer and dryer in the basement, but those went in the first garage sale. He was also big on the boob tube, a man who grabbed the *TV Guide* as first choice out of the Sunday paper. He liked the crime shows, always interrupting the characters' dialogue, predicting the outcome. And he usually fell asleep in that big brown chair. That's how I remember him, slouched into the first deep snores, his belly lifting and deflating with every breath.

Dad disappeared one summer night when the stars were burning too bright. With a suitcase of clean laundry and a wallet of life savings, he rolled off in a pale blue Pontiac smelling of aftershave and a brand-new haircut. The sad thing was nobody was sad.

I found Mom that night sitting on the screened-in porch listening to the nervous fritter of crickets and june bugs. Her sagging eyes were staring into the darkness, her forefinger rubbing the edge of a jelly glass filled with whiskey. She was still trembling from the fight, the big one, the last one.

"Your father has gone off to find himself." She turned and looked at me for the longest time. "He wants to make believe he's someone else."

I stared back at her, wondering what to say. Mom's hair was matted by the constant rubbing of sweaty hands. She looked like she was planted in that chair and was destined for an all-nighter.

"Can I get you anything?" I asked.

"Maybe it's better for him," she said, "better for us."

That's Mom; always looking at the upside. The world could be ending and Mom would be ecstatic about the extra days off work. Dad was probably halfway to St. Louis by then. It sort of reminded me of the time the dog ran away, either he would come back in a few days or we'd never see him again. And a guy like that, who just turns his back on his past, who is willing to give up everything he's ever known, any guilt he might have will fade as fast as the sunrise, any sorrow will be drowned in a row of empty Budweisers.

T R A C Y

TRACY came over looking exceptionally hot. Her blond hair was severely brushed and a fresh coat of pink lipstick smothered her lips. Wearing a tight lavender sweater over a black Wonderbra, a deep purple miniskirt, hot pink tights, and a candy bead necklace, she looked like a character in a new wave video. The sweater had shrunk in the wash or I suppose that's deliberate because Tracy had her belly button pierced, and now every outfit centers around her latest ornament of rebellion. I'm sorry, but I have to protest any social statement that costs twenty dollars at the mall. She sat down beside me, took a pair of scissors out of my Teletubbies lunch box, and started cutting pictures out of *Seventeen* and *Jane*.

"You looked wigged," she said.

"I met Mom's new flame tonight."

"The fireman?"

"The astronaut. She's like glue stick on this one. I think it might be serious."

"My mom always says the new one is serious."

"Your mom is trying to choose between lobster and salmon, my mom is looking for a sale on tuna fish."

Tracy dipped into her purse for a cigarette. "Where'd you go on your first date?"

"A church social catered by the Ladies of Tupperware. They served Kool-Aid."

"Well that's a new one." She laughed. "What about the old man? Do you like him? Is he cute?" She found the Camel Lights, pulled one out, pushed it between her swollen pink lips. Tracy has the most amazing lips.

"I told you. He looks like an astronaut."

"Yeah, but what else?"

"He's a sex-crazed fundamentalist."

"There's no commandment against sex." Tracy lit her cigarette, blew out the match.

"Yeah, but it's implied, isn't it?"

"Maybe." Tracy shrugged. "Where's your brother?" She looked around, like it would even matter. The boy is absolutely brain-dead.

"He's in the basement practicing feedback."

"I don't hear anything."

"He has his headphones on."

"Is he still in self-purgatory?" Tracy sucked on her cigarette, blew the smoke toward the window, then leaned closer toward the door, as if to hear him calling for her, which he wasn't, because my brother is lost in a far off galaxy aboard his own private *Enterprise,* slipping into one black hole after another with absolutely no intention of ever coming back.

It wasn't long ago when David was still struggling through his aftershave years, scraping peach fuzz from his face with an antique razor Mom found at a garage sale. Standing in front of the mirror, he'd always nick the tender skin around his newly formed Adam's apple, then press a tiny square of toilet paper on the wound and wear it around the house like some badge of maturity, proof that puberty had struck, that he was acquiring the power of virility, the strength of masculinity, the ability to elicit desire from the opposite sex. His soft blond locks crept down to his shoulders, and the girls at school started using up precious phone time. And then, after a fierce breakup in the ninth grade with some slim-waisted hair goddess named Alice Garvey, he withdrew into a hurricane of stimulants. First some big dips into marijuana and LSD, and now his new resting place, the warm loving arms of heroin. Cobwebs have grown over dark corners nobody ever dreamed existed. Brown circles have blossomed under his wild blue eyes. He quit shaving, the phone stopped ringing. What started out as a flight from boredom has become medical bliss. He's only a reflection of his former self. Tracy's crush is just one more dent in his armor.

"Do you have any homework?" I asked.

"I have a big report due on youth-culture fiction."

"How's it going?"

"Slow. I haven't even gone to the library yet. It's gonna take forever, but I have to finish it. My life will be over if I don't graduate." Tracy bit into one of her nonexistent fingernails. "It's so hard to concentrate, knowing the curse is still hanging over us. When do you think it's gonna happen?"

I shrugged my shoulders. Everyone at school is totally freaked about the senior curse. For the past eight years, a member of the senior class has died before graduation, which is now only two weeks away. Nobody has died yet, but I can think of a few candidates. Last year, on prom night, a member of the soccer team was driving barefoot after a kegger and his car kissed the guardrail and did a couple 360s over the embankment. The year before, a girl drowned in the quarries. There was a suicide once, back when I was in junior high, but the rest have been car accidents as far as I can remember. We've been drilled to death about drinking and driving by the school counselors. Last week the state police brought in the crash simulator so we could have a real taste of blood and guts, but when they showed the movie and the car exploded into a ball of flames all the kids in the auditorium cheered. They show the same film year after year. What do they expect?

At last year's sobfest the class president read a poem that went something like "don't try to understand everything because some things don't make sense." I can't tell you how many times someone used that as an answer in one of my classes this year. It should be our yearbook motto. My classmates are starting to place bets on all the losers, but deep inside they're getting sorta paranoid as well.

"I just hope they don't cancel graduation," Tracy said. "I'd feel so empty being thrown into society without a ceremony."

Tracy and I were making collages for our fanzine *As My Stomach Turns*, an after-school project that has ballooned into a major time consumer. We started it when the school paper didn't report the shooting in the parking lot: Some sophomore math whiz went postal and blew away a few hall monitors and a gym coach before ramming the gun into his own mouth and making spaghetti of what was left of his mind. He was part of a crowd that sprinkled angel dust on their Wheaties, the spiritual leader of some thick-headed glue-sniffing satanists who liked to mutilate small animals after school. Tracy recorded some interviews on her Walkman and transcribed them word for word, then pasted them into columns and illustrated it with snapshots she took with a disposable camera. (I liked the one of me standing in front of the gunman's locker.) We made a bunch of copies at her mom's office.

Our little rag has a total circulation of about fifty copies, but that's only because we're more interested in designing the next issue then distributing the old one. Xeroxing is a drag. Our current issue is centered around astrological predictions about the curse, which we obtained from a psychic in California by dialing a 900 number, and our only letter (from a guy!), which asked, "What should I do if I get a boner in the shower after gym class?"

Tracy and I combed the yearbook twice trying to figure out who might be gay. We tried to match the handwriting to signatures from last year and the year before that. Nobody has ever come out of the closet at our high school, because they know they would die. Which means our next issue will be highly controversial. Tracy says we might get suspended and then we could protest and become international media darlings for taking a stand against the evil marauders that run our school system, but my fear is that a few morons will use the issue as an excuse for a witch-hunt and there might be some misguided bloodshed over rumors and innuendo. Either way the sensational aspect of our coverage will ensure another sellout, and we'll be stealing as many free copies from Kinko's as possible in a matter of days.

One night I was baby-sitting at the neighbor's house and they have a computer, so *As My Stomach Turns* went global over the Internet. We posted X-rated letters to rock stars. Tracy lied and said she was a sixteen-year-old model itching to lose her virginity. One guy wrote back and asked her to describe the girls' locker room at school. Which of course she did—in livid detail, going off on this huge lie about having her underwear stolen and spending the entire day without panties. Tracy's posting got about a zillion responses from perverts all across the universe. At first she was real proud of her sexual conquest, but later she started getting paranoid and told me some creep followed her through the lingerie department at Wal-Mart.

I've known Tracy since forever. When we first met on the grade-school playground she shined like a quarter you find under a couch cushion. She bleached and ironed my hair, got me started as a vegan, and sorta introduced me to sex. Tracy was the beacon that helped advertise my desire. She has an amazing ability to get attention, but she's more talk than action. Tracy is a chronic serial crusher and gets the itch to ditch a guy as soon as she snags him, but if she feels even the slightest tremor of lust she's on the phone burning a hole in my eardrum. Talking is her Valium.

"Did you hear that?" Tracy asked.

"Hear what?"

Tracy tilted her ear downward, as if she were trying to tune in some fading frequency leaking from the basement. "Nothing, I guess." She went back to work with the scissors.

Tracy's had a major crush on my brother since the day her eyes landed in his airport, and his constant indifference is the equivalent of throwing petroleum on a brush fire. Her devotion has synthesized into a cultish groupie eulogy. She arrives on our doorstep with the regularity of a commuter train, acting like some lost princess looking for her misplaced shoe. David somehow fits into her tidy mold of an alternative grungelord. Mr. Depression, however, is not into girls right now. He'd rather stay in the basement like some musty old troll and snort heroin with his stupid friends. The four of them sit around a card table every weekend playing gin rummy, blasting their records so loud the neighbor told the cops it was drowning out his lawn mower.

The deck of playing cards is as dirty and frayed as everything else in the basement. One day, the jack of spades tore in half, and so my brother taped it back together, then tore up all the other jacks and taped them up too. So now everybody knows you have a jack, but not which suit. It's the stupid kind of logic he and his friends have for everything. My brother's been keeping score since they were fourteen, and at a penny a point he thinks he might be able to retire at thirty-four. And sometimes I wonder if it's not true: not the retirement, but the fact that they'll still be down there fifteen years from now.

"Is your brother gonna start a new band?" Tracy asked.

"He says he doesn't want to go commercial."

"Starting a band would be a sellout?"

"According to him, the only way to be alternative is to not participate."

Tracy leaned her head back toward the door in that solemn gushing hush, so respectful, so willing, way of hers.

My brother's old band, GLOOM, broke up after the lead
singer hung himself. Joey's suicide note declared his weakness
his greatest strength, and his death his greatest artistic achieve-
ment. The guy had dirty ears, that's all I remember about him.
Tracy never got over it and still whispers whenever she talks
about him.

"So what's going on with you and the mechanic?" Tracy
asked. "Have you taken the car in for a tune-up yet?" She
worked the scissors around a dELiA*s supermodel, anxious for
some lurid details, which I usually made up for her carnivorous
needs.

"I did a drive-by in Mom's car."

"And?"

"He had his shirtsleeves rolled up."

"That's it?"

"What did you expect?"

"Well at least you could've stopped for gas."

"I can't get gas every day!"

"Why not? It's a free country."

One day we were bored out of our minds, cruising aimlessly
in Tracy's bug when the mechanic rolled up beside us at a stop
light in his awesome purple Charger. I was sitting there checking him out, so Tracy beeped her horn and finally he glanced
over at me. We locked into a momentary stare, but when the
light turned green he burned a fat patch of rubber right beside
us. It was definitely one of those looks like, someday, somewhere, something's gonna happen, but when I stopped for gas
a few days later he acted as if I were the invisible girl.

Tracy started arranging her cutouts on a sheet of newspaper.
The cover story was about that plane crash in Wisconsin. The

headline said 75 SECONDS OF HORROR! in bold type. I stared at the picture of the wreckage. The little pieces reminded me of dinosaur bones found in an archaeological dig. A woman's dress hung from the limb of a tree, and I wondered if I could ever be that woman, my remains indistinguishable from hundreds of others, lost in the debris, scattered forever.

"We gotta go," Tracy said, "the movie starts in ten minutes." She tossed the glue stick into my lunch box, stood up, brushed paper scraps from her skirt and picked little pieces off her sweater, then grabbed her blue suede jacket. I got up, twisted the sleeves of my black sweater around my waist, checked to make sure we didn't forget the cigarettes, then turned off my bedroom light.

Tracy drove us to see *Kurt and Courtney* at Meadowbrook Mall. She had an ancient red Volkswagen Beetle. Her dad left it behind as part of his guilt trip when he ran off with the hussy of his dreams. All my dad left me were his scratched-up bongo records, embarrassing leftovers of his beatnik hour. Her feet barely reached the pedals, but she drove like a maniac. The mall was only five minutes away. Tracy made it in three. We smoked the rest of my allowance in the parking lot before going into the theater, and I was swimming in it by the time we bought our tickets.

We flashed our stubs to the usher and slipped between the folds of red velvet curtain. My eyes took forever to adjust and I wobbled through the darkness. Tracy marched up front so the screen was right in our face. The place was pretty much deserted, except for a clan of jocks munching popcorn toward the back.

The movie started, and before long my stomach started doing flip-flops, so I went and sat in the lobby. The carpeting had one of those geometric patterns, and I tried following it, like a race car speeding through a video game, but when the room began to swallow itself I ducked into the bathroom and leaned over the toilet bowl for a while. There goes potluck. Afterward I felt a million times better, bought a small Coke to rinse my mouth, then went back into the theater.

Tracy was front and center, curled into a fetal position, squeezing her toes, her glassy eyes in deep focus. I handed her my Coke, and she grabbed at the straw like someone who just came back from the moon, sucked the whole thing down to one last giant gurgle of ice and backwash, then gave it back to me. I set the cup on the floor.

The movie made me sad. Everyone in it looked like they'd just survived a train wreck, everyone except Courtney that is. Tracy, however, was on a whole other wavelength. She studied the movie as if it were some kind of how-to manual for boys with guitars strapped over their waists. She felt destined to marry one and took every opportunity to learn more about them, as if she had cast herself in her own movie and was just waiting for the shooting to begin.

When the house lights came on, Tracy rubbed her hands on her tights, then tucked them under her sweater. "I'm freezing," she said. I followed her up the aisle and through the lobby, squinting in the harsh light, careful to avoid the mob of head-shaved jocks crowding into the john. We crossed the barren parking lot. A thin layer of dew covered the cars, and the lights hanging overhead shone with the lonely afterglow of day's end. Tracy's VW started right up and she cranked the heat. The weed was wearing off, the depression starting to simmer, slowly creeping back into my life. Tracy turned on the windshield wipers, lit a cigarette, then the whole car started shaking and tilting like that little girl's bed in *The Exorcist*. I rolled down my window and saw a pack of all-stars rocking the rear bumper of the car. Their leader tapped on Tracy's window. She rolled it down and blew smoke in his face.

"What the fuck is your problem?" Tracy asked.

"Evening ladies." He waved the smoke away. "Looking for an adventure?"

"What are you—a travel agent?" she asked.

"There's a killer party around the corner. You should come check it out." He winked at Tracy. "Unless, of course, you two just want to be alone."

"We'll think about it." Tracy rolled up her window, then looked over at me with one of her sex-crazed looks. The quarterback batted the top of the VW and danced back over to his blue Camaro. His cronies piled in one after another.

"Uh-uh," I said. "No way."

"Let's just check it out," she said.

"I'm tired of trolling cul-de-sacs. He isn't even my type's most distant relative."

"Maybe he has a cousin or an uncle. Think of it as shopping, if nothing fits we'll go somewhere else."

I just wanted to go home, but Tracy had her own ideas, following a car full of drunken football players through silent subdivisions. I pleaded, but Tracy insisted, so we ended up at some shabby duplex behind a strip mall called Willow Creek. The apartments were faux ski lodge—very seventies. You could hear the music in the parking lot, an empty keg was lying at the bottom of the stairs, a fresh puddle of puke on the first landing.

"Looks promising," I sneered.

Tracy held my hand as we entered the apartment and dragged me directly toward the kitchen. Green Day was blasting. A few murky lights burned in the corners. There were lots of bodies, lots of sweaty faces, but nobody I recognized from school. A few rocker sluts were pinned down in the corners giving face to major scum.

"Where are we?" I shouted over the music.

"It's some poor idiot's idea of a bachelor pad." Tracy shrugged her shoulders and pointed to the Bud babe poster taped to the wood-paneled wall. "I think his name is Chuck or something."

"And what kind of guy is Chuck?" I asked.

"Probably an ex-football player who didn't get a scholarship and is now doing time at the local community college, trying to get his grades up for a shot at state college in two years. Maybe he'll even make something of himself as long as he doesn't kill anybody in the meantime." Tracy went straight for the refrigerator, which was scarfed down to a torn open twelve-pack of Milwaukee's Best. Tracy took two and handed me one. I scanned the room and began sorting through the dismal prospects. The problem with jocks is that they're as interchangeable as a lightbulb. And when they look at you at this time of night it's with only one purpose in mind. Gross.

"Tastes like Lake Michigan," Tracy said, looking at the can.

I opened the freezer. "What do you suppose is in those plastic containers?" I asked.

"Body parts," some fathead said, butting in to grab a beer.

"How come looking around this room gives me very little reason to doubt you?" I asked.

"Maybe you watch too many scary movies," he said.

"Or lived them." Tracy began drifting away.

"Where are you going?" I asked.

"Over there." She pointed toward the couch. "You still know how to scream don't you?"

I leaned against the kitchen counter trying to look ugly when Mr. Body Parts started hitting on me like I owed him something for the beer. He was an overweight musclehead with little or no understanding of his incredible lack of charm.

"I'm Chuck. Who are you?" He let out a huge belch, popping his beer can open one-handed.

"I'm gone." I turned and headed for the bathroom which, thank God, nobody had puked in yet. I sat on the toilet, but was totally pee shy. My limbs felt cold, and I wished I was at home curled under my sheets sleeping toward tomorrow.

Someone hurriedly pounded on the door, so I pulled my corduroys up, flushed the toilet, and opened the door. Chuck comes barreling in and locks the door behind him. Fatso's got a big drunken date-rape grin leaking across his face, and he's acting all superior, like maybe he's too good for me and I'm about to get lucky.

"We meet again," he says.

"We say good-bye again." I tried getting around him, but he stood in the way and stared at my breasts like the vacant drooling ape that he was.

"What's your hurry?" he asked.

"Well, to be honest, I really don't want to watch you pee."

"What are you doing in here then?"

"I'm not here, it's just an illusion." I tried getting past him again, but he pinned me against the towel rack, pressed his nose against mine to advertise his psycho capabilities.

"You feel like you're here to me." He laughed, as if the two sides of his brain were trying to outwit each other, then he grabbed my waist and pushed his against mine, so I could feel the merchandise packed under his denim jeans. He looked compulsive and prone to irrational ideas, someone who might prove very harmful if not handled with the utmost care.

When his hand slid up my arm and over my breast I stepped back and kicked him in the balls as hard as I could. He buckled under, screamed "Bitch!" like it was my fault or something, and crumpled onto the floor. He grabbed my left leg and tried to tackle me, so I stomped on his head with the other one. I didn't care what happened to his face. I just kept on kicking him over and over again until shiny drops of red blood dotted the linoleum floor. When his hand finally loosened its grip, I unlocked the door and excused myself. I hurried through the kitchen, found Tracy on the couch squeezed between the quarterback and some other steakhead. A pyramid of empty beer cans were stacked in front of her.

"Tracy," I said. She pretended not to hear me.

"Tracy!" I screamed. "We have to leave!"

"Whatayatalkinabout?" the quarterback slurred, as if I was spoiling all his fun. Tracy looked up at me, and I gave her the death stare.

"Guys," she said, slapping their knees, "it's been fun, but I have to go meet my boyfriend."

"She's your boyfriend." The quarterback pointed at me. "The carpet muncher. The queen of shag."

Tracy stood up and walked toward the door.

"From one homosexual to another," I said, nodding to him, then kicked the coffee table, and the pyramid of cans came crashing down into his lap.

"Hey you stupid bitch"—he brushed the cans off his legs— "who the fuck do you think you are?"

I gave him the bird with one hand while Tracy grabbed the other and pulled me toward the door. When we were outside Tracy started laying into me about how I always had to ruin everything. When we got into the car she gave me the silent treatment royale: Her Hole tape cranked and the Berlin Wall between us.

As we drove away I saw the fathead I made love to in the john come running out into the parking lot with a paper towel caressing his nose, obviously looking for *moi*. I had a good laugh. Several yahoo companions were right behind him. One of them pointed at our car while the rest loaded into an Oldsmobile that quickly backed out behind us. As we drove up Woodward Avenue past Wal-Mart, I looked back and saw *Revenge of the Steakheads* tearing up pavement behind us. Tracy was puttering along and I wondered if I should warn her or just let the circumstances fly.

It was only seconds before they pulled up beside us. Chuckie started throwing half-empty beer cans at Tracy's car. She rolled down her window.

"What the fuck's your problem?" she yelled.

"I'm gonna kill that bitch!" Fatso leaned out of the car and pointed at me, his other hand still nursing his nose. I prayed for a telephone pole to chop off his head.

"Who is that pig?" Tracy asked. I squirmed in my seat.

"I think his name is Chuck or something."

"What did you do?" Tracy rolled up her window.

"He busted into the john looking to play Mr. President, and when I said N-O he got pushy, so I was forced to suppress his advances."

"Did you mace him?" Tracy sped up the car.

"No, I kicked him in the balls!"

"That's it?" She looked into her rearview mirror, shook her head back and forth slightly, a tiny grin lifting from the corner of her lips. I could tell she was starting to side with me. "You should have flushed his head in the toilet and gave him a swir-lee." She took her foot off the acclerator, rolled her window down again. The carload of monsters roared up beside us, their fearless leader still leaning out the window.

"Hey you!" Tracy yelled. "The guy in the backseat!" She pointed at him. An onion-headed dweeb peered out the rear window. Tracy slowed down even more, but not enough for them to do anything stupid, just enough so she didn't have to scream.

"You know what your boyfriend's problem is? He got beat up by a girl!" She laughed.

"He's not my boyfriend," he said, and then spit at her, which of course, because of the wind, blew back in his face.

Tracy just lost it. She cracked up so hard I thought we were gonna crash. She rolled her window shut and made a sharp right into the far end of the empty Wal-Mart lot. The girl is a genius.

I looked back and saw the Oldsmobile spinning through a U-turn and into the lot behind us. They weren't giving up. Tracy kept her eyes peeled straight ahead, bouncing over speed bumps, determined now to lose them. But they were insane. Within seconds the deathcar rolled up and kissed Tracy's car from behind. We were knocked forward. Tracy reached for her seat belt and I did the same.

"Those assholes are really starting to piss me off!" Tracy made a sharp left out of the lot and raced back down Woodward to Sixty-third Street. The deathcar was still on our case. Tracy turned left onto Sixty-third, trying to cut them off at the light, then sped toward the highway entrance. The deathcar ran a red and followed, then roared up right behind us and rammed the back end of the car again. I looked back and saw their laughing faces and started to get real scared.

"Who are these creeps?" Tracy looked into the rearview mirror again. She seemed oblivious to the terror now racing through me. She was totally in control, not a speck of fear, pure kamikazee. I was starting to sweat for real, this was like some scary movie about to get ugly.

"What are we gonna do?" I asked.

"Look and see what's in the backseat," Tracy said. "Maybe we can throw something back at them."

I unbuckled my seat belt, leaned into the backseat, and waded through the dirty gym clothes and empty water bottles.

"Why do you have a car battery back here?"

"I was supposed to drop it off for recycling. Bring it up here. I think I see the recycling bin now."

"What?"

"Just get it!"

I reached for the battery, and lugged it into the front seat. The thing weighed a ton.

Tracy smiled at me. "Okay, this is what we're gonna do." She took a hit off her cigarette, flicked it out the window, turned down the music. "I'm gonna slow down and let them crawl up on our ass. When they get too close you pop out the sunroof and drop them a valentine, okay?"

"This?" I shifted the battery on my lap.

"Here they come. Ready?" She started rolling back the sunroof. A fierce blast of wind swept through the car and whipped my hair around uncontrollably. I turned, crouched on my left knee, and pressed my back against the dashboard. Tracy slowed down, and sure enough those assholes snuck right up like a bunch of lazy thieves smelling opportunity.

"Now!" she said.

I lifted the battery up to my chest, then stood and heaved that sucker with two hands as hard as I could. The battery's flight wilted instantly, but it clipped the front end of the hood, bounced once, and then crushed the windshield. The deathcar skidded slightly to the right, then slowed down and stopped in the middle of the highway. I prayed for a huge semi-trailer to come and flatten them like a pancake, but it limped slowly over to the shoulder like some half-dead roadkill looking for a less hostile place to die.

Tracy pulled my pants leg. "What happened?"

I crawled back into the car, flopped down into my seat. Tracy closed the sunroof, looked over at me.

"It fucking totaled the windshield." I looked back the other way to make sure they weren't still behind us.

"Whoa," she said, trying to find them in her rearview mirror. Tracy looked over at me, cracked a huge smile, grabbed my knee, and shook it. "See! Now wasn't that fun?" She exited the highway and tailored a route using back roads all the way home.

I had a sinking feeling that we hadn't seen the last of our new friends and that it wouldn't be long before they crawled out of the sewer for a sequel. My body was shaking in this hyper-euphoric way, like I'd just jumped out of an ice-cold river and there wasn't a towel, but there was also a constant fearful shine, like when you're on the swing set and you've gone a little too high.

"I might have just killed someone," I said.

"Well at least you got that out of your system."

"Tracy! It's not funny."

"They fucking deserved it." She looked into her rearview mirror as if they were still there. "They could have just as easily killed us!"

"I think we just made a big mistake," I said. My stomach was turning against me.

Tracy flipped over the tape. "If those fuckers ever mess with you again, I will get crazy," she said, trying to reassure me. "I'm serious." She flicked her lighter and waved it around. "I'll light their fucking hair on fire!"

THE FIELD

ALL through the night I churned in and out of consciousness, tracing the outline of my room, making sure everything was still in its place. A white noise rang in my head as if both ears were covered with seashells. My mouth was a paste factory. Menstrual cramps were rising from the dead.

I rolled over and played it all back in dreamy slow motion: the car battery rolling over the front hood and shattering the windshield, the wind slapping my face, the car fading in the distance. I crunched my fingers tighter around my pillow and tried to knock the guilt out of my conscience, but it only doubled and then tripled. In a few fast seconds the next chapter of my autobiography had accelerated to a dangerous new level. Certain the doorbell would start ringing any moment now, I kept glancing out the window for mysterious cars curling down the cul-de-sac. The backs of my knees felt sore, the muscles around my shoulder and neck were killing me. I called Tracy, but her line was busy. Figures.

I swallowed more aspirin and tried coaxing myself to sleep by tuning into an airplane, following its drone across the black sky, listening as it evaporated into the horizon. But my eyes wouldn't close. I was fluent with visions. I couldn't turn them off.

My mother was at the other end of the hallway, sipping bourbon and fornicating in front of late-night television with the man from Mars. What I couldn't hear I imagined. Her occasional outbursts of passion seemed to rattle through the air vents like some haunted sexual demon lurking in the walls.

I kicked off my blankets and crept down the staircase into the kitchen, then opened the sliding glass door and slipped out into the yard. Cool air swarmed around my ankles, my feet were baptized in the slippery grass. A full moon bleached the star-spangled sky. The wind lifted the sound of freight trains rumbling across the open prairie, of cars racing along Sixty-third Street, of crickets mating in the weeds.

Beyond the long sharp fingers of the pear trees was a canopy of scraggy lilac bushes that marked the borderline of our yard. The branches looked like twisted wizard canes creeping up from some Gothic underworld deep below the surface of clover-choked grass. Across the street was a patch of waist-high weeds and small sickly trees—a big stoner hangout called The Field. Stuck between developments it's a place where the soil sinks and water collects into small marshlike ponds, an uninhabitable place in a county where people rely on sump pumps to keep their basements dry. It used to be full of scaly brown toads that looked a thousand years old. Pheasants and ducks once nested in the spiky underbrush, but even the mosquitoes have disappeared since the bulldozers arrived.

On the corner of the lot stood an ancient willow tree. Its drooping branches hung like a firework frozen in time. I clawed the ridged bark of the fat black trunk and pulled myself up, then climbed steadily from one branch to the next. No matter how many times I'd done it before, it still made me nervous.

This tree was as old as the days of horse-drawn carriages, back when boys carried rifles and girls wore long white dresses with high collars, when Indians were as common as mailboxes at the end of driveways. I come up here to listen to the wind shake the leaves. It's hypnotizing. I almost fell off once.

My legs wobbled with caution all the way to the crest where three branches cupped into a perfect seat high above the yard. Fireflies sparkled in the moon shadows. Clouds slipped into one another. I found a satellite and watched it sink into the horizon. The sky seemed wide open. I wished I could fly from tree to tree, from town to town. I wished the sun would never rise, that the world would just go on sleeping.

Only a few days away from graduation and suddenly a bad shadow is clipping at my heels. The cops will probably be here any minute. Why do I listen to Tracy?

My legs were superwobbly. I felt shaky and unsettled, so I climbed back down, then jumped from the lowest branch and fell into the grass. The ground was hard as rock. I crossed the lawn to the outer ring of evergreens that marked my grand-mother's property line. She lived behind us in a small farm-house. Grandma moved here when this town was still a swamp-filled county of tumbling barns and sticker bushes. My dad grew up in that old white house. She sold a good portion of her land to the developers who built our house. I guess Dad got some kind of deal as part of the arrangement, and that's why we're neighbors. Grandma's yard was lush with flower beds, fruit trees, and most recently a sixteen-foot satellite dish. In the dark it looked like a flying saucer had crashed behind the house. Grandma put it together herself from a kit she ordered out of some magazine. It sucks down every channel in the universe.

I wouldn't really call her an inventor, but Grandma sure liked her experiments, especially anything to do with electricity, but sometimes her formulas got a little out of hand. Once she tried harnessing lightning with a flagpole rigged to the chimney and nearly burned down the house. Her basement was packed with glass beakers and wild electro gear from the days of Dr. Frankenstein. Wires run in every direction. There are jars filled with condensors and transistors and a whole shelf of various glass bulbs. She's always melting or dissecting something. Mom blames her weirdness on Dad, says that since his vanishing act Grandma has veered even farther off center, that her universe was no longer balanced, and a lot of other mystical New Age whatchamacallit.

I don't know what lured me over to Grandma's sky vacuum, but that's where I found her, sprawled out in the grass. She scared the hell out of me. I thought she was dead.

"Grandma!" I jumped down and shook her. I was in a panic until she mumbled a few incoherent phrases. She carried on as if she were having an argument with God at the front gates of heaven or something, probably trying to renegotiate her lease or being stubborn and refusing to go in without her remote. I couldn't understand a word of it, so I shook her gently.

"Grandma, Grandma," I sang sweetly. She was in her own

world, far away from mine, bartering for a better deal on whatever it was she wanted. I wondered if I should leave her there
and let the sunlight sober her up, or call an ambulance and have
the men-in-white rush her away to a world of narcotics and life-
saving drills, or just hold her hand and let her be. Grandma's face
was crinkled as a dried-up riverbed. Blue veins thick as bones
bulged through her skin. Her white hair was wild and unkempt,
sorta matted to the top of her head. She was wearing a man's
shirt and pants. When I put my hand on her forehead, her blue
eyes slowly fluttered open, then stormed into consciousness.
Grandma jerked up and grabbed my hand. "What the hell?"

"Grandma, it's me, Chrissie. What are you doing out here?
I almost stepped on you!"

She twisted her neck slowly, as if to uncap the mystery, or
at least try and get the facts straight. "I was having trouble with
the reception, so I came out here to check on my soup bowl.
That's when it happened, a total ambush, must have been three
or four of them, faces like bandits . . . I think . . . maybe I . . ."
She shook her head, trying to remember.

"You got mugged?"

"No, no." She leaned up and brushed herself off. "Rac-
coons. They came right at me."

"Were you bit?" I lifted her up onto her feet, checked her
skin for abrasions.

"They scattered into the trees," she said, pointing.

"C'mon, let me help you back into the house." I wrapped
my arm around her shoulder.

"I think it's time I got a fence." She limped back toward
her little white house. I opened the screen door for her.

"What were you watching?" I asked.

"Huh?" Grandma was still a little out of it.

"On television. What were you watching when the juice went out?"

"Something about the end of the world."

"What did they say?"

"I don't know. I missed it," she said. "You want a glass of milk and a little cherry pie?" she asked. And then she sang— "I've got some Cool Whip!"

"No thanks, I'm kinda sleepy."

"You never say no to Cool Whip."

"I know but I—"

"Why were you out wandering through the yard in the middle of the night?" Grandma pressed her nose against the screen.

"I couldn't sleep," I said.

"You got the swimmy eyes of boy trouble," she said. "What's your fella's name?"

"I don't have a fella," I said.

"Yeah, but you got one in your sight. I can tell. A girl doesn't wander around the yard in the middle of the night without boy trouble blowing through her head. There's only one cure for restlessness," she said, her head swaying back and forth. "Men are a terrible disease, but I suppose you gotta learn that for yourself." She looked up at me. "You want me to leave the porch light on?"

"Nah, I like the dark."

"Just like your father."

"What?"

"Indian blood. I'm sure of it."

"What are you talking about?"

She slammed her door and locked it twice.

H I S T O R Y

I started having these weird dreams about Indians when I was in grade school. Whether chasing wild chickens or getting drunk with white men, it seems as if I had some previous life in this neighborhood. The land our house occupies was stolen from the Pottawatami Indians in 1832 by a guy named Pierce Downer. He scrambled out here when the frontier was opened by the U.S. government's success in the Black Hawk War. There was enough gruesome slaughter on both sides to make an awesome miniseries, but nobody really gives a shit about Illinois in Hollywood.

After an all-nighter at Fort Dearborn, the Indians were coerced to trade the land on this side of the Mississippi River for the land on the other side of the Mississippi. The Indians shook hands with their new friends, packed their bags, and spread out into the Black Hills, only to find General Custer creeping through their territory a few hours later. My guess is that the senior curse is directly linked to something that happened a long time ago and that the spirits we're dealing with carry a nasty grudge.

My grade school was called Indian Boundary because the land it occupies was once a place that marked a neutral zone of commerce between the two nations. Indian Boundary Road has a notorious curve with three oak trees lining the bend. It's become the local dead man's curve. There's at least one every summer, and the corpses are usually young and almost always intoxicated.

Our family has been living here since forever. My grandma once owned a tavern on the corner of Sixty-first and Dunham. She had a television before there was programming. Locals came from miles around for Friday night wrestling and ten-cent beers. There's a scrapbook in Grandma's pantry with a zillion black-and-white photographs. People sat outside on picnic tables and ate corn on the cob, waiting for the sun to go down. It was so folksy even Norman Rockwell would puke.

The place deteriorated in the fifties when happy hour became the home of unhappy social outcasts. One night someone got stabbed in the bathroom, and a few weeks later a fire finished off what was left of that sagging beer-soaked timber.

Grandma's mom's mom was the wife of a German blacksmith who never came back from the Civil War. She took up with a local Indian trader and had a second litter. I'm a descendant of that batch. I'm not quite a half-breed, but I'm just as much an Indian as Cher.

The porch light went out. I crossed the yard and slipped back into the house. The astronaut's spaceship was still parked in the driveway. I went upstairs, pulled the covers over my head, and curled up into a ball, hoping tonight never happened and tomorrow would never come.

BREAKFAST

I woke up with a splitting headache. The sweet scent of coffee and buttered toast drifted up the staircase. I could hear Mom tooling around the kitchen. My hair still smelled of smoke and my hands had grease on them and then I remembered the car battery and the shattered window and wondered if the police had already stopped by. I was a little nervous about heading downstairs, but at the same time, I was anxious to know, *Did I kill them?*

The morning light had the appearance of a sky viewed from the bottom of a sink filled with dirty dishwater. The aspirin bottle was nearly empty and I had the sinking feeling that I've eaten practically every one. I drifted down the stairs, floated into the kitchen. David was still sleeping. Mom was reading the *Tribune*.

"There's coffee made. Do you want some toast?" She jumped up, ready to serve me, like some bored waitress hungry for a two-dollar tip. I made her sit back down, got the coffee myself, added two scoops of sugar and lots of milk.

"How was the movie?" she asked.

"Okay."

"What was it about?"

"A murderette rock star and her road-kill husband."

"I don't want you seeing so many R-rated movies!" she said, trying to be a mother.

"Mom, life is an R-rated subject."

She knew she was full of shit, but she had to go through the motions, being a dad as well as a mom. I didn't dare ask her what she did last night; just the thought of her twisting in the sheets with that lanky astronaut sent shivers up and down my spine.

"Anything good in the paper?"

"Just the usual mayhem. I sure miss Monica."

I took a big gulp of coffee, sat down at the table. My throbbing head simmered into a steady grind.

"There's a big oil fire down in Lemont." Mom held the paper up so I could see the picture. "That's probably the first time Lemont ever made the front page." She laughed to herself, then set down the paper and took a deep breath in preparation for another page from her scrapbook of life lessons. They've been getting progressively religous in tone ever since she started her interplanetary voyages with the astronaut. Mom's been invading his cosmic world, anxious to make a splash landing.

"I have a surprise," she said, pushing a black velvet ring box in front of me. "Open it."

I lifted the tiny lid, and sure enough there was a crystal-clear rock set in a wide silver band sparkling like the first day of

spring and all the promises of life. I looked at the wrinkles
fanning out from the corners of my mother's eyes, swallowed
all the smart-aleck comments perched at the edge of my
tongue. If there was ever a time to contain my inner thoughts,
this was it.

"Dan wants to marry me!" she said, hardly able to breathe.
She drank the last of her coffee, kept her eyes locked on my
facial expressions, waiting for the slightest inkling of approval.
I felt a million rain clouds perched right above my head and
lightning blasting the perimeter. When I stared into my
mother's eyes they were a dreamy mixture of hope and mushy
thoughts about her man of the hour. I fast-forwarded into the
future: new neighborhood, new school, new Dad, new rules,
new life.

"Does David know about this?" I asked.

Mom shook her head.

"Does Dad?"

She shook her head again.

I was the testing ground, just like the sands of Nevada.
Scorched earth.

"It's kinda sudden," I said, not wanting to break Mom's
heart. I wanted her to be happy. I had to tread softly. I didn't
dare flinch or say what I felt. I picked up the box, looked at
the diamond carefully.

"It's awfully big," I said.

Mom nodded and cracked a little smile, like she was embarrassed.

"Does it fit?" I asked. "Try it on."

I pushed the velvet box back toward her. She quickly
opened it and slipped the ring onto her left finger, then held

her hand toward me. We both stared at the glittering rock. The basement door popped open and Sir Gloomster shuffled into the room, smelling like three days ago. He slumped into his chair, reached for the Frosted Flakes, and filled a bowl. Mom got up and fetched the coffee.

"Notice anything different?" I asked him.

He looked around the room as if the wallpaper had been replaced overnight. He tasted his cereal, trying to recognize a new flavor, shrugged his shoulders, gave up.

Mom poured his coffee so her hand was right in his face. He couldn't miss the diamond. David stared at it, and at first he didn't say anything, not even a smirk. I tried to imagine what new damage was settling into that frostbitten skull.

"That's a nice ring, Mom." He took a sip of coffee. "Where'd ya get it?"

Mom took a deep breath. "Dan gave it to me. He wants to marry me."

My brother stared into the bottom of his cereal bowl like he wanted to stick his face in it and drown. He looked up at Mom, tried seeing her, but obviously couldn't.

"So what are you gonna do?" he asked.

"I haven't decided."

"Do you love him?" I asked.

Mom took a deep breath and exhaled slowly. "I don't love him like I loved your father. It's different, but I'm a different person."

"Don't you have to break up with Dad first?" David asked.

"I haven't said yes yet." Mom leaned away from the table. "I just thought I'd mention it, to feel you guys out a bit."

"How do we feel?" I asked.

"Hesitant," she said. Mom's face was torn wide open. She reminded me of one of those paintings of little girls with incurably sad eyes. "I want to ask a favor of you."

"Uh-oh," I said.

"Will you go to church with me tomorrow morning?" She smiled a big happy smile, like, *won't it be fun?*

"You're getting married tomorrow?" David asked.

"No, no, no, no. Dan invited me. I just don't want to go alone."

I slouched in my chair, hoping this was just a phase and not some new Bible-thumping mom I was going to have to deal with.

"Do we have a choice?" David asked.

"I'm giving you one aren't I?"

"What time is church?" I asked.

"Nine o'clock," she said.

"In the morning?"

"It'll be over before you know it. Who wants more toast?"

DAIRY QUEEN

A timid sun bled through the hazy overcast, the air smelled like compost and bug spray, humidity made everything nice and sticky. Six-foot weeds drooped over both sides of the narrow bike trail, some with fuzzy tops, others draped with wide brown leaves. The path's chalky white gravel rattled against the rusted fenders of my Western Flyer. I coasted along, trying to digest the concept of a new dad. I guess I never realized that your relatives could evolve. Tossed into a soap opera with a total stranger, it'll be like camp that never ends. Here a dad, there a dad, everywhere a dad, dad.

The path cut through a swatch of weeds and spilled into the Green Knolls shopping mall, a geographical armpit at the corner of Sixty-third and Main. Foremost Liquors had windows full of white paper signs advertising cheap six-packs and discount vodka. Lawn ornaments and pallets of wood chips surrounded the doorway of Ace Hardware. A soldier was smoking

a cigarette outside the armed forces storefront. The Hobby
Barn was barren. I stopped at the Dairy Queen and filled out
a résumé, used Tracy as a reference, Mom as a past employer,
and listed boy watching as one of my hobbies. I have to get a
job this summer. Money is my only hope.

Outside the DQ I saw the mechanic's purple Dodge Charger
parked beside the Steakhouse. I pedaled across the lot and
locked my bike around the flagpole, then went inside. The
room was decorated with wagon wheels and various other
western memorabilia. There were picnic benches in the center
room and a smoky effervescence that reminded me of a camp-
fire. Bobby was sitting in back, hunched over a hamburger and
fries. I picked up a yellow plastic tray and slid it down the silver
rail, stopping in front of the beverage dispenser to fill a paper
cup with iced tea. I paid the cashier, then took a deep breath
and slowly cruised his table. His face was buried in some gear-
head magazine, totally absorbed by an article about tires. Long
dark bangs curled over his skyscraper cheekbones, his lips were
purple, as if he'd been sucking on a Popsicle. He didn't look up,
so I sat down across from him, squeezed some lemon over my
ice cubes, stirred the citrus into the tea with my pinkie finger.

"Mind if I sit here?" I asked. When he looked up I stared
right into his eyes, just like the first time we met, hoping he'd
pick up where we left off.

He shook his head and mumbled "mmmnbrgh" with a
mouthful of food, then picked up the ketchup bottle and shook
more onto his plate. Twisting off the white cap and smothering
his fries, he reminded me of a European movie star playing a
cowboy. His elegant features clashed with his rough gestures.

He seemed somehow miscast as a mechanic. He was too shiny for his job.

I took a long sip of tea while watching him chew. "I saw your hot rod outside. You drive here? I mean, you only work across the street." I pointed with my thumb.

"I know," he said, still trying to swallow. "Habit, I guess." He took another bite of his hamburger, stuffing in french fries between gulps of soda. Now he was looking at me, noticing me, trying to place me. He had the biggest brown eyes. "How did you know I work across the street?"

"I buy gas sometimes."

"Oh yeah, you're the girl who always buys a dollar's worth of gas. I didn't recognize you without your car." He took another bite, looked back at his magazine.

I started to feel annoyed. He wasn't making this very easy. I thought that once I laid myself on a silver platter for him, he'd respond with a few lines of yummy tease or scalding words of affection, but instead he acted like a Frisbee had landed beside his beach blanket and now he was annoyed about having to stand up and throw it back. He took another bite of his hamburger and turned a page of his magazine.

"I heard the world is gonna end in a few days," I said.

"Oh yeah?" Bobby didn't look up. "Where'd you hear that?"

"My grandma saw a television special about it. She's got a satellite dish so big it picks up channels you've never even heard of."

"So why is the world ending?"

I took a sip of my tea, thinking up an answer. The clouds

shifted and a scrap of sunlight fell through the window. I looked outside and remembered the petroleum fire. "I think it has something to do with that fire down in Lemont," I said.

Bobby looked up from his magazine like he didn't believe me but was still willing to play along.

"Have you seen it?" I asked.

"No." He set down his burger and leaned back in his chair.

I reached over the table and took one of his french fries and dipped it in the ketchup. "I sure would like to know what the end of the world looks like."

"I doubt anyone would stop you," he said.

"Yeah, but I don't want to go by myself," I said. "Don't you want to drive down and see the end of the world?"

"I can't right now." He shook his head. "My lunch hour is almost over."

"What time do you get off work?" I asked.

"I gotta close tonight."

"What time is closing time?"

"Around ten," he said.

He looked at me kind of funny and I felt a big raspberry sprout on my cheeks.

"You don't seem very scared," he said.

"Of what?"

"The end of the world."

"Oh that." I looked over and saw a couple of guys from the party last night walking up to the counter. My heart leapt into my throat. I quickly turned my back to them. I wasn't sure if they were friends of Chuck or not, but I didn't want to stick around to find out either. I looked back at Bobby.

"My life is sort of complicated right now," I said.

"More complicated than the end of the world?"

I looked over and saw the boys pushing their yellow trays down the silver rail, the last in line was the onion-headed one.

"Sorta," I said, wondering what to do, looking for the nearest exit. "I just remembered something." I got up from the table. "I have to run. I'll tell you about it later." I hurried outside, unlocked my bike, and rode as fast as I could over to Tracy's house.

PANIC

THE Nelsons' lawn was completely overgrown; the gutters were packed with leaves; all the planters were still potted with last year's dead flowers. I stashed my bike behind the bushes and rang the doorbell. Nobody answered, so I tossed a pebble at the window upstairs. When the door finally swung open, there was Tracy, still in her flannel pajamas, holding a can of ginger ale in one hand and a cigarette in the other; her hair was working a serious hangover.

"All right already," she said.

The house was a mess, several dirty plates were stacked on the paisley-shaped coffee table. Twice as many dirty glasses ornamented the counter space. Clothes were strewn randomly about, and the carpet was buried in newspapers and magazines: the usual chaos. The television was barking a Live Action Report from Chopper 9 about the petrochemical fire in Lemont.

"They say people can see the smoke all the way from downtown Chicago," Tracy said, pointing at the screen. I fell onto the couch, fanned myself with the *TV Guide*. Tracy plunged into the big orange vinyl chair opposite me.

"I did it," I said.

"Did what?" Her eyes were glued to the television set.

"The mechanic."

"You did the mechanic?" Tracy sat up and pressed her cigarette onto a dirty plate.

"I asked him out on a date."

"No way."

"Just now at the Steakhouse." I took a cigarette out of Tracy's pack. "We're gonna go see the fire in Lemont tonight." I struck a match and lit a cancer stick.

"Well, that sounds like a hot date."

"It was my idea. I just thought it would be fun, you know, at least we'll be parked."

"Why don't you go to a motel, at least there's a bed," she said, mimicking my voice.

I threw the *TV Guide* at her, propped my legs up on the coffee table. "Have you heard anything about those guys?" I asked.

"What guys?"

"Last night!"

"What's to hear?" She laughed to herself. "Action speaks louder than words."

"A couple of Chuckie's friends showed up at the Steakhouse while I was talking to Bobby. I freaked out. Do you think I hurt him?"

"I hope so."

"What if they come after us?"

"Did you give him your phone number?"

"Of course not."

"Well how are they gonna find you? He doesn't even know your name."

"It's a small town. They'll ask around. They might see your car!"

"If they see my car they better duck." She pulled me out of my chair. "C'mon, you're making me nervous."

We went upstairs to Tracy's room. The shades were drawn, the bed unmade. Red shag carpeting smothered the floor. Her walls were buried with posters of various rock stars and CK boys posing in their underwear. There was a scratched-up desk and matching dresser, both originally painted white, now graffitied with swirling rainbows of Magic Marker. She had a collection of old dolls and stuffed animals piled in the corner, which seemed like an installation dedicated to her past life, and a corkboard with souveniers of one-night stands pinned one over another as a celebration of her present one: buttons, bottle caps, concert tickets, dead flowers, even torn-open condom wrappers. Her dresser was brimming with stolen merchandise. Tracy was a kleptomaniac at the mall.

There were three library books stacked up on the edge of her desk. "What's with these books?" I picked up the top one.

"I have to do that stupid report," she said.

"What's it about?"

"Look at the covers." She nodded toward them.

"So?"

"They all have clouds on them, don't you think that's weird?"

"So what's your point?"

"That is my point. How many points do I need?"

"I've heard of *Generation X* and Bret Easton Ellis, but what's this big fat one?"

"It says he lives in Bloomington, Illinois. Not much happens here, so you can just imagine what it's like in Bloomington. He probably has a lot of time to write. Check out the author photo. He's kind of cute in that thirty-something English teacher way."

"What's with the bandanna? Is he in a gang?"

"I'll speculate on it in my report," she said.

Tracy clicked open her tape player and slipped in her sleazy-listening compilation. Mancini meets Manson is how I would describe her latest musical tastes. She calls it wife-swapping music.

"What do you wear to a fire?" Tracy opened one of her drawers and pulled out one item after another: short pants, leather pants, suede skirts, cotton T-shirts. In the next half hour Tracy put together just about every ensemble imaginable, then suddenly turned around with a devilish smile. "Why don't you wear nothing at all? Just a long gray raincoat and high heels."

"I'm not a slut!"

"Yeah, but you want to be." She laughed knowingly, holding up the brown suede halter top she swiped from her mom's collection. "You're as horny as a Prince song."

"Should I make the first move?" I asked.

"Only if you have to."

"When will I know?"

"You stare at that fire long enough and you'll know." Tracy handed me her baby blue angora sweater. Its hairs stood on end from static, wiggling with a cosmic life all their own. "Wear this," she said. "It works every time." She held the sweater over my chest. We both looked in the mirror.

"Do you think he's Mr. Right?" I asked.

"I think he's Mr. Right Now!" Tracy laughed.

MY MECHANIC

TIME crawled away with the helpless tempo of a traffic jam. The summer light seemed to last forever. Lingering through dinner, it was one of those never-ending sunsets that delayed drive-in movies—a swollen haze of pollen and air pollution, a glowing gaseous orange with wispy vapors of purple and blue. I cranked up the volume of my hair, did some overtime in the t-zone, then painted my nails ultraplatinum. It was a night meant for high-beam gleam. I wanted to sparkle like waxed chrome under streetlight. After a couple of preliminary failures I settled on a sliver of metallic mascara and a light dusting of pearly pink iridescent powder. Clothing is never easy and it took several dress rehearsals, but I decided on blue jeans, a white T-shirt, and Tracy's fuzzy blue sweater: something old, something new, something borrowed, and something blue.

It was only nine o'clock but I couldn't wait any longer, so

I went downstairs and told Mom I was going over to Tracy's. I hate to lie but sometimes the truth is just impossible. I took the shortcut through the field, which was not a good idea, because it was dark and the weeds were sparking my fertile imagination. I'm not usually a paranoid person, but lately everything's been getting a little weird. Whenever I'm alone I feel like I'm waltzing through a crime scene.

I landed at the Chicken Shack and ordered a small Diet Coke, then sat on a stool by the window and watched cars come and go from the gas station across the street. My mechanic went car to car, washing windshields, pumping gas, sometimes disappearing into the garage for a can of oil. He looked so sweet with that little pink rag drooping from the back pocket of his black jeans. Pushing a broom under bright white fluorescent light, he was my own private movie star.

I watched him wheel in the oil can cart, roll up the air hose, and measure the gas in storage below the surface with a long yellow pole until finally, a little after ten, the overhead lights were turned off. The gas station was closed. I coated my lips with a fresh dose of lip gloss, tossed my paper cup in the can, and strolled across the street. I tapped on the garage window and saw my mechanic turn with surprise. He walked over to the door and fumbled with the lock.

"You made it," he said, then turned his back to me and bent over the sink to scrub his greasy hands. He wore a tight, gray short-sleeve T-shirt and black jeans pegged over steel-toe boots.

"Nice place ya got here." I leaned against the Coke machine

and slid my hands into my front pockets. The garage smelled
like old motor oil. Hundreds of crushed cigarette butts littered
the greasy black floor like little white bugs.

He turned off the water and dried his hands with a white
paper towel. "It's a job," he said, shrugging his shoulders, then
dropped the towel into the trash. "Where do you work?"

I stumbled on that one, my head swimming with responses.
He turned around and pounded some quarters into the cigarette machine. "You got a job or you some kinda psychokiller
chick who preys on gas station mechanics?" He picked up his
cigarettes and tore open the cellophane wrapper.

"Heard about me, huh?" I gazed at my shoe.

Bobby tapped the cigarette pack against the palm of his hand,
then tapped out two cigarettes and offered the first one to me.
I pulled it from the pack, slipped it between my lips. He seemed
tense under all that cool, his face didn't seem as sure as his
demeanor. I could tell there was some vulnerability under all
that swagger. Silence swelled and sucked up all the air. He
clicked open his silver lighter and ignited its blue and orange
flame. I dipped my cigarette into the fire and inhaled. The
lighter fluid was so rich it tasted like I was smoking gasoline.

"So, you still want to go see that big fire?" he asked.

My right leg took on a life all its own, swinging forward and
back. I twisted my arms into a pretzel. "Isn't much else to do,"
I said. "You got any other ideas?" I flipped my hair away from
my face.

He looked over my body and I returned the compliment.
Bobby closed the bottom drawer of the desk with his knee,
then turned around and grabbed his black leather jacket from

the coatrack. "The fire it is." He turned off the office light, opened the door for me, then locked it behind us.

The purple-flake paint job on his '78 Charger glittered like the prizes in a gumball machine. The interior reeked of history—dead smoke and worn leather—somehow it already smelled familiar to me. This was my vehicle into the next chapter. I just wanted to be there, now.

My mechanic latched his seat belt and told me to do the same. He started the engine, pushed in a cassette, and the car burst to life. Nine Inch Nails crept out of the stereo. When he pressed the accelerator the first thrust of gasoline exhaust ripped through the tailpipes and the engine's sweet rumble turned to a fearsome roar. He shifted into gear and peeled out of the lot.

I slipped my hand under the black vinyl seat, feeling for trinkets like lost earrings, bottle caps, or torn condom wrappers, anything that might help me look into the past or predict the future. My mechanic concentrated on the dark road, shifting through the gears, both hands locked on the wheel. Sometimes his eyes squinted or his head tilted, as if he saw something lurking in the black perimeter. He looked so intense driving. I was speechless.

Bobby's face was dominated by large lips and long sideburns. His nose was twisted as if it had once been broken and never reset. A thick purple vein bulged from his slender neck, his flat chin balanced the twitching muscles of his jaw. He looked powerful and reckless, like somebody who's already tasted the pavement.

I rolled down the window, folded my arms over the windowsill, and let the warm wind blow through my hair. The scenery slid by like an ambient movie, a zillion frames a minute;

white lines disappeared under the car, warped reflections peeled over the windshield. I saw the pink eyes of an opposum hunched over a dead raven in the gravel shoulder of the road. It stared into the headlights, then scampered behind the guardrail and into the weeds.

We passed the Johnsons' abandoned farmhouse. The windows were broken, the weathered gray boards buckling. A large white billboard stood out front announcing the new development. The entire farm was mapped into tiny green squares with a black line snaking around the land in S-shaped curlicues. Mr. Johnson died last year and his farm was instantly swallowed up by some big-time developer. The cornfield already had sewer lines and streetlights in place. It all happened so fast, it seemed like they were waiting for him to die.

"So where are you from?" I asked.

"How do you know I'm not from here?"

" 'Cause I've been here long enough to know."

He turned and checked me out but didn't say anything. I tipped my head back out the window, crossed my legs, and stared at his reflection in the windshield. The curve of his lips reminded me of the bending hills of a roller coaster. I closed my eyes and felt myself sliding down the first hill.

"I'm from Southern Illinois."

"What brings you up here?"

"Work."

"They don't have any gas stations down there?"

"Yeah, but they already have mechanics. Everybody down there is a mechanic. Up here everybody is a businessman. Businessmen don't know shit about cars. They bring them to me and I charge whatever the hell I want."

"You came up here to take advantage of us?"

"It's called the redistribution of wealth."

"Are you a Marxist?"

"Are you a spy? You sure ask a lot of questions. What do you know about this fire?"

"Saw it on TV," I said. "Biggest celebrity in the area, I guess."

We came over a ridge, and the fire everybody's been talking about came into view. A huge petrochemical storage tank was on fire, and its plume of thick black smoke had burned a hole in the sky for about two days now. From across the canal it looked like the earth had cracked open and the entrance to hell was slithering from its hideaway. Fireboats projected lazy streams of water onto the steel casings of the nearby tanks. Old tires and half-sunk houseboats floated beside a rotting pier that sloped down under the oil-slick water.

"That fire is bigger than I expected. It looks so greedy and wild, like an angry ghost or something."

"You believe in ghosts?" he asked.

"Sure, why not?" I looked over at him.

"You believe in UFOs too?"

"There wouldn't be UFOs if UFOs didn't exist," I explained.

Bluff Road was clogged with double-parked vehicles. People were slouched on the hoods of their cars drinking beer. Everyone's face was shaded with an orange glow, reflecting the fire's leaping light. Bobby couldn't find a parking spot and ended up being detoured into a long snaking line of sight-seers rambling over the canal bridge. A few people stood outside the lawn mower repair shop, one of them pointing up into the sky.

"Do you suppose that stuff's dangerous?" I asked, sorta hallucinating in the swirling whirlwind of red, white, and blue emergency lights.

"If it was, somebody would of said so by now."

"Yeah, but what if they didn't? Maybe there's something in those clouds?" I leaned closer to the glass to get a better look. "I don't trust anyone these days, especially the government."

"How do you know you can trust me?"

"That's a risk I'm willing to take."

"So you're in a car with a complete stranger, but you're worried about some little puffs of smoke drifting off into outer space."

"Hey, it's not as illogical as you make it seem, and those aren't little puffs, they're big black balls, thank you." But then I had to think about it for a second. "You have to trust your instincts. What's right is right," I added. "You're flesh and blood, who knows what that stuff is." The cassette tape ended and it felt like a bell announcing the end of round one.

"Isn't it weird how everyone seems so drawn to death and destruction," I said, peering through the glass, trying to trace the trail of smoke. "Look at all those people!"

"It's sort of religious actually, if you think about it, like passing in front of an altar"—he wiggled the gearshift—"people suddenly feel lucky to be alive." My mechanic stared into the oncoming headlights as if he had a long line of thoughts racing to a finish line.

"This is way better than religon," I said. "Church is so boring. And who'd want to go to heaven anyway? I can't think of a worse party."

"Who said you were invited?"

I looked at him with a strange sense of amusement, something I never felt with anyone else. He had the weirdest point of view and I can't believe he mentioned religion; what a trip. Staring at him in this light he carried a warm alienish glow, and I wanted to believe he was an angel.

"Do you believe in God?" I asked.

"If there wasn't a God, God wouldn't exist." He looked over at me and smiled.

Touché. What could I say? My mechanic was a spiritual *Meisterbrau,* a greasy white prince, a minister of machine parts. I felt myself twisting into a chain-link mesh.

The music blended with the wind and the roar of the Charger. The interior was colored by the oncoming blur of passing cars bending through the wide curves of the two-lane road. We drove past the UNOCAL petroleum refineries. Tiny white bulbs traced its skeleton of black and silver pipes. Three musty pill-shaped train cars were parked behind the chain-link fence. Power lines looped over the tree line, disappearing into the Black Partridge Woods.

A thick toxic scent filled the car. My breath was shortened and my face started burning. I tried to rationalize the concept that we had just driven through an industrial accident, that I might be the victim of toxic agencies already chewing through the fibers of my internal organs, that this was probably the beginning of the end. I rolled up the window, checked my reflection in the glass and the huge black plume of smoke pushing farther into the heavens.

"This must be the biggest thing to happen around here since the night they fried John Wayne Gacy," I said, shifting on the bucket seat and trying to imagine myself in the electric chair: the first surge of electricity; my hair frying; my fingernails turning black and peeling back; my eyeballs popping out of my head.

"Did you go to that too?"

"No. That was a long time ago. Where are we going?" I asked him.

"My garage." He coasted through a yellow light. "I gotta check in with some friends before we go anywhere else." He looked over at me. "It'll only take a minute."

"Where's your garage?"

"A few more lights," he said, pointing ahead.

We sped through Lockport. Old brick bungalows and tar papered shacks lined Archer Avenue. The waterfront became a faint glow and then a shadow behind us. I saw a cigar tree, remembered smoking the long finger-shaped seeds when I was in grade school and getting sick as a dog.

Bobby accelerated through another yellow and I felt myself getting too comfortable in the seat, worried this date was going nowhere. We turned off Archer Avenue and wound through a thicket of trees and empty lots across the river from Stateville Penitentiary. In a hollow of trees stood a two-story wood building with the garage door open. A couple of guys were inside working on a dented-up race car. The car had big wide tires and was painted black and orange with a large white number 89 on the door. Behind the garage was a junkyard full of mashed cars. Two large German shepherds paced behind a fence, barking madly, their white teeth snapping, their paws pushing against the wilting chain-link.

"What's that?" I pointed into the garage.

"My ticket out of here," he said.

"You a race car driver?" I asked.

"Sometimes." He shut off the engine. The car sputtered to a choking death.

"Where do you race?"

"Wherever they'll let me." He punched open his door. "Stay here, I'll be right back."

He got out and pointed at the dogs. "Jonesie, Maxie, down." He snapped his fingers and the dogs dropped to all fours, then trailed him along the fence line, their tails wagging softly behind them. Bobby said something as he approached his two friends and they all started laughing. One of them looked back at me in the car, then they all disappeared into a doorway. I leaned against the window and stared at the prison across the water. At night, the complex looked like the dark side of Disneyland. All I could think about was all the creepy-crawlies locked inside.

When David and I were kids Mom took us to a prisoner art show. It turned out one of the painters was one of Mom's classmates from high school. I had never seen a murderer before and remember being very excited. He was wearing leg chains and what looked like blue pajamas. He reminded me of those handsome Nazis in old war movies, so that even his good looks seemed sinister. At the time, Mom said he was a basketball player who suffocated a cheerleader with a pillow. We found out several years later that he was gay and that this girl had laughed at him when he couldn't get it up, that she threatened to tell the whole school about it. The weird thing is, I can't remember anything about his painting.

A rusting BEWARE OF DOG sign dangled from the barbed-wire fence surrounding the junkyard. The sharp white teeth and shiny black eyes of the dogs cruising the yard were giving me the creeps. I turned up the Nine Inch Nails tape, closed my eyes, and tried to sink into Trent's melodrama.

My mechanic turned out to be more complex and glamorous than I expected. I knew he seemed out of place pumping gas on the corner of Sixty-third and Main. The way he talked, his body language, almost everything he did seemed to hold a hidden agenda. Even now he has to have some secret meeting with his pals.

Whatever they were doing, it seemed to take forever. My stomach was practicing flip-flops. The car was getting cold. The dogs kept pacing, occasionally barking at a bird or some other critter crawling through the weeds. I locked my door as a precaution, then leaned over and locked Bobby's too. The place reaked of urban legends.

Finally, mystery date popped out of the clubhouse and made his way back to the car. When the door burst open, the interior light and car buzzer set the dogs off in another barking frenzy. Bobby clicked himself into the seat belt, started the engine, and backed out of the driveway onto the narrow road. He shifted into first and squealed the tires. My head whipped back against the black vinyl seat.

"What kind of car was that?"

"An 'eighty-four Chevelle with a four-fifty-four engine. It's a beater, but it always starts." He laughed to himself.

"I can't believe you race cars," I said. "Why didn't you tell me?"

"I didn't know you were into cars," he said.

"You never asked. Can I come see you race sometime?"

"I don't see why not. It's a free country last time I checked."

"How long have you been racing?" I asked.

"Since ninth grade."

"How old are you now?"

"Twenty-six."

He didn't ask me how old I was. In fact, he didn't ask many questions at all. It was like a long game of truth or dare, only he kept responding "truth." We crossed over the tracks and rode along Industrial Drive, a semideserted stretch of land bordering the petrochemical plants. Across the street stood a trailer park of bread box homes haphazardly spread among patches of waist-high weeds. We passed an old red barn that was tilted sideways with its roof sagging in the center. THE TIME IS NEAR was painted on the roadside wall in fading white letters.

"So how'd you learn to be a mechanic?" I asked.

"I had a beater in high school; a 'sixty-eight Fairlane. One day it started bleeding oil all over the driveway. I didn't have any money so I got the bright idea to take the engine apart and try to fix the leak. The first thing I learned is that it's a lot easier taking apart than putting back together." He laughed to himself.

"So being a mechanic is sorta like solving a crossword puzzle, right?"

Unsure of the comparison, he looked at me like I was interpreting too fast. "Every car is different. They all have their own personalities."

"Your friends, are they mechanics too?"

"I met those guys from towing in wrecks off the highway.

One night we sat down and killed a twelve-pack and they
started telling stories about racing up in Wisconsin. They built
that car out of used parts from the yard." He made a left turn
and was quiet while glancing into his rearview mirror. "The
original driver kissed the wall and cracked his ribs. They needed
a replacement and I needed the bread, so I volunteered."

"Is it dangerous?"

"Driving that shitbox is like square-dancing with a chain
saw." Bobby stared forward with the determination of a
mailman pushing a cart of letters, sucking down one cigarette
after another, riding a nicotine wire. From time to time he
would space out, and you could tell he was watching his
own movie, that he had a multiplex in his mind with never-
ending showtimes. My brother was the same way. What is it
with men and their glamorous brooding monster within?
Bobby's face launched a thousand words but it was still
Scrabble as far as I was concerned. Staring, waiting, I wal-
lowed in his silences.

"Your family, they live around here?" I asked. "They all
crazy as you?"

"You think I'm crazy?" He turned the music down a hair.

"I think you're unusual. Tell me about your grandfather.
My mom says men are always like their grandfathers."

"My grandfather?"

"Yeah."

"Well, his name was Charley and he lived right near the
Kentucky border. Neighbors used to call him Batman because
bats would fly around his house at sunset. The big walnut tree
in back was full of them." He turned and looked over at me
in a kinda boyish excitable way. "He was an ambulance driver

and a bootlegger, made most of his money running moonshine into East St. Louis and up north through college towns."

"No way. Your grandfather?"

"Yeah, sure."

"Was he in the Mafia?"

"No."

"Was he a good guy or a bad guy?"

"Depends on whose side you're on."

"Did he ever kill anybody?"

"Just himself." Bobby shifted, and the car sped faster. "He was racing in a cow field at some county fair. I guess that's all there was in those days. His brakes failed and he kissed the wall. The car went airborne and flipped upside down. The fuel tank burst." He stared out the window. "That car had the aerodynamics of a yellow pig."

"Oh my God, that's horrible."

Bobby lit a cigarette. I leaned against the door and watched him smoke, wondering if he was aware of his own mythology. His body language said he'd visited that novel a million times before.

"Don't you ever get scared?" I asked.

"Driving makes me feel like what's behind me is always getting farther and farther away."

I wanted to ask him what he was driving away from but was intimidated by the thought of old girlfriends, so I avoided the issue. "Does your dad race cars too?" I asked.

"My dad disappeared over in Vietnam." He looked out the window, as if Vietnam was just beyond the next patch of trees. "He's MIA. They never found him."

My endless questioning had just driven the wrong way down

a one-way street. I stared at my fingers, kept crossing and un-
crossing them, rubbed my palms together, traced the heart line
with my finger. "Do you think he's still alive?"

"Sometimes I like to think he just drifted off from the war
and made himself invisible, but I doubt it. I don't have much
to go on, just some photographs really."

I didn't know what to say. Bobby was suddenly distracted
by a rush of memories. I could tell by his blank stare that they
were pouring in. "My dad was in the army too," I said. "He
came back, but then he left again."

"Where'd he go?" Bobby looked over at me again.

"I don't know. He said he was leaving. Mom said okay, and
that was that."

Bobby's head tilted back and forth, as though he disagreed
with what I just said. More silence chased our flowering friend-
ship, but at least we finally had something slightly in common.
I wanted to ask him about his mom, but I was worried I was
asking too many questions, but then went on asking anyway.
Silence=death.

"So how do I learn to race cars?"

"By driving. You'll have to get behind the wheel and scrape
a few walls to find out what it's all about. There's no text-
book."

"Can't you give me a few tips or something?"

"Every driver has their own style, their own way of holding
the steering wheel." He shifted in his seat. "On a small track
you gotta work the walls, everything gets congested down low,
too many inexperienced Joes trading paint and getting stuck in
the infield mud. Sometimes I spend half the night joyriding
under yellow flags. There's no fast way through the corners,

you just throw the car sideways and try to keep it from sliding out of control. It's a gut feeling, you have to chase your instincts. Maybe it seems sort of risky, but right now it's the only hope I've got," he said.

"What do you mean?"

He gunned the car forward. "I don't want to be pumping gas when I'm twenty-nine."

I tried to imagine where I'd be at that borderline but then stopped in front of a huge billboard that said DON'T GO THERE.

"You got any plans?" he asked.

Most of my plans went no farther than next weekend. I glanced out the window, saw my reflection in the glass, the flaws, the imperfections. "Sometimes I think I want to be an actress," I said. "A serious actress portraying the heroines of modern literature."

"Have you ever been onstage?" he asked.

"Not yet." I tipped my head out the window. "But sometimes I feel like my life is a movie."

"PG-13," he said.

"What?"

"Your rating."

"How do you know? You haven't seen the whole movie yet!"

Bobby laughed. I could tell he was at ease with me, that we had definitely passed GO.

"So how'd you stumble into such a glamorous occupation?" he asked.

"During Career Day at school I told my counselor that I wanted to be a farmer, maybe take over one of these old cornfields around here. He whipped open some charts and said that in the near future farming would decline by fifty percent, but the need for entertainers would rise by fifty percent. His words of advice were—'Don't be a farmer, play one on TV.' "

My mechanic pulled onto the fire road that surrounded the limestone quarry and parked beside some overgrown bushes. "I know a place where you can see the fire," he said.

I got out of the car and followed him under the highway bridge. The creek smelled like sewage and there was garbage everywhere. Rusted drums were scattered along the water's edge, shredded plastic bags laced the dead tree limbs reaching from the bank. We passed a doorless refrigerator spray-painted 6-6-96 and a shopping cart filled with rain-soaked newspaper flyers.

Bobby carried a green army blanket under his arm. It wasn't the magical place I always imagined, but it would do. Trudging along the creek bed, ducking under the occasional low-hanging branch, my eyes slowly adjusted to the darkness. I started feeling a little sweaty and nervous, thinking, *Wasn't this how all young girls died?* Following his shadowy frame through the thick black underbrush, I tried to convince myself he wasn't a mass murderer.

We came to a ridge that overlooked the canal. In the distance was the glowing site of the petrochemical fire. The panic of emergency lights seemed quaint from this viewpoint. My mechanic spread out the blanket, then took my arm and guided me down beside him.

"It's not beautiful, but it's something," he said.

It was beautiful in an end-of-the-world kind of way. Emer-

gency lights swept the perimeter. The bridge was a shimmering
wake of headlights that wormed over the canal. It looked like
some cheap UFO footage for a low-budget sci-fi movie.

Bobby smelled like grease with a hint of crushed leaves. He
blended in perfectly with the environment. He was so quiet at
times I felt like he wasn't even there. We both lay under the
stars, watching the planes line up on the horizon, waiting to
land at O'Hare.

"Make a wish," I said.

"I wish I had a real car," he said.

"You already have two cars."

"I'm tired of risking my neck in rebuilt wrecks scraped off
the highway. That lawn mower might look impressive, but
looks don't win races."

"Well, if they did, you'd win every night," I said.

Bobby threw a stone up at the sky. "It won't be long, you'll
see. I'll be racing full-time with a sponsor. Once I get a faster
car and start racing bigger tracks I'll be winning bigger prizes.
I'm tired of getting my ass kicked at Santa Fe."

Bobby was totally focused on drowning in his glamorous
fate. Racing seemed like a life-or-death situation for him, as if
tonight was just another speed bump on his yellow brick road.

"It's probably just a matter of timing," I said. "Somebody
will need you, just like you need them." My mechanic was
getting melancholy, so I sat on top of his waist and pushed his
shoulders down to the ground, then traced the outline of his
lips with my fingertips.

"Is this where you bring all your girls?" I asked.

"Yeah," he said nonchalantly. "They're all buried over
there." He nodded toward the weeds.

I looked into the weeds. "You're just kidding, right?" His hands crept under the folds of my sweater, over my T-shirt, and traced the outline of my bra. He rubbed me gently, his hands pressing my breasts. I leaned down and kissed him, slow slurpy kisses, running my fingers through his dirty hair. He rolled me over onto my back, pressed his lips to my earlobe. "That's for me to know and you to find out," he whispered, then stood up and started to walk away.

"Hey wait a minute," I said. "Where are you going?"

"Ssshhhh!" he disappeared behind some trees into the inky darkness. I could hear him rustling through the bushes, circling the perimeter. If he was trying to be creepy it was working. I heard footsteps approaching, so I grabbed a rock just in case.

My mechanic crouched down beside me. "Close your eyes," he said.

"No way," I said.

"Close your eyes!" he insisted.

"Why?"

"Just close them."

I looked at him and he was smiling. It wasn't a dangerous smile, it was a fun smile, a smile I was willing to trust. "Okay," I said and closed my eyes.

He pressed his fingers between my lips and placed a wild raspberry into my mouth. The juice squirted over my lower lip and ran down my chin. We made out fiercely, an all-out face mosh. His hands roamed all over the map. My eyes clenched shut while he fumbled through the buttons of my sweater, one after another, finally pulling it over my shoulders. He reached under my T-shirt and unlatched my bra. It loosened around my shoulders. He kissed my breasts, his warm

tongue spinning around my nipples, his lips gently sucking. I
was about to die. He shifted farther down south and kissed my
tummy, rimming my belly button. He started to unbutton my
blue jeans, and that's where I stopped him. It wasn't easy. I felt
like a field of dry grass caught in a lightning storm.

"Whatsa matter?" he asked.

"I'm not ready for a full-scale invasion." I pulled his hair,
lifted him up to my lips and kissed him. He pressed against me,
his hips swaying like a snake, rubbing his crotch against mine.
I squeezed my thighs around his leg.

"Do you have any condoms?" I asked.

"Don't worry," he said, "I won't come inside you." And
then he kissed me again.

My passion surfed a tidal wave of emotions. I wanted him
desperately, but I started to worry about AIDS and herpes and
crabs and all the other nightmares of health class. I started
thinking about my mom's early pregnancy. When Mom and I
had our little talk she warned me about this trick. "Guys have
about as much control over their sperm as God does with a
tornado," she said.

"Are we or aren't we?" he asked.

"Let me check my bag." I cracked open my bottomless
purse. Under all the wadded-up dollars and loose change was
a stick of gum, my lip gloss, and "I'm not so stupid after all,"
one priceless prophylactic. "Here." I handed it to him.

And then a strange beeping sound started ringing in his pants.

"What the hell is that?" I asked.

"My beeper." He pulled it out of his pocket and checked
the number. "C'mon," he said, grabbing my arm. "We gotta
go."

"What do you mean?"

"It's the garage . . . it's part of my gig. There must be a wreck on the highway."

His mood changed with the speed of a light switch from red-hot lover boy to distant repairman. He got up and went to pee in the woods. I looked down at myself briefly, then scrambled to pick up the pieces. My eyes slowly refocused, my ears lost their buzz, my heart drained of intensity. Bobby was already somewhere else, but I was still shaking from his first visit.

He took my hand and walked me out of the woods, then drove me home in one of the heaviest emotional silences I've ever experienced. I tried to reignite some passion in the car, but that was about as useful as the fire hoses downstream. I lay my head on his shoulder, but our distance could be measured in miles.

"Do you ever see the dead bodies?" I asked.

"Sometimes," he said.

"What do they look like?" I looked over at him.

"Sometimes they look like the morning after in hell." He stared into the oncoming headlights. "And sometimes they just look like they're sleeping."

His cool detachment made me pine for him even more. I wanted to cuddle up into his arms and tell him my life story, to listen to the soft gurgle in his voice explain how a carburetor works, but there was only an unbearable silence.

When he dropped me off in front of my house, he kissed me good-bye and promised to call tomorrow, but his voice already sounded like a long-distance telephone call.

I walked up the driveway, pushed my key into the slot, went

into the kitchen, and poured a glass of water, then slithered upstairs to my room. Comforted in the familiar scent of my dirty bedsheets, I burned with the afterthoughts of a dream date, wishing he were pressed against my backside, his arm curled over my tummy, his heartbeat thumping against mine.

SUNDAY MORNING

MY mouth was pasty, my eyes were fuzzy, I looked like total shit. Anxious about tomorrow and regretful of the past, Sundays are like New Year's Day once a week. I strapped on my body armor, then slipped an old lace dress over my head, squeezed into last year's prom shoes, found some jewelry in the Cinderella box—a fake diamond necklace from Grandma and a silver bracelet from what's-his-name.

Mom was dressed, and I must say, looked stunning for eight o'clock in the morning. I was still reeling in from my date, and Mom was already casting her line. She wore white, so I wore black. Staring into the mirror I tried to arrange my hair, but it was too matted and tangled, so I settled for a wide-brimmed hat and a hairbrush to work the split ends in the car.

"We're not going to a funeral," Mom said, giving me the once-over as I came down the stairs. Her makeup was so carefully drawn she looked airbrushed, and I could tell she had a push-up bra under her dress.

"Just say the word and I'll stay home and read the paper." I wanted her to back off and remember who was doing who a favor.

"There's oatmeal on the stove," she said, pointing toward the kitchen. Her voice was already less hostile, almost concessional, and I knew she was grateful.

I flopped some oatmeal into a bowl, added milk and honey, then spooned it up as quickly as possible, sucking down coffee between every bite. Mom was watching me, watching the clock, bouncing off the wall with anticipation.

"It's so nice to see you all dressed up . . . so pretty, so . . ."

"I feel like a call girl in this oufit."

"For once you don't look like your brother." Mom poured me some orange juice, pushed the glass and a big brown vitamin across the counter.

"Are you saying I'm butch?" I asked between spoonfuls.

"I'm saying it's nice to see my daughter in a dress. Don't you want to look pretty?"

"I want to look smart."

"Take your vitamin and let's go. I don't want to be late. Lutherans are so judgmental."

"What about David?"

"He's not feeling good," she said, heading for the door.

I knew she was leaving him behind on purpose and that once again I had to be the guinea pig. I chugged my juice and followed Mom outside.

The garage smelled like lawn mowers and gas cans and was cluttered with things that didn't work: the bike with the flat tire, the hose with the hole in it. Mom started the Ford and backed out. I brought down the garage door, brushed my hands, then plopped into the front seat beside Mom. We rode along in silence. Too tired to talk, too tired to listen, my head was still spinning from last night's sleeplessness. It didn't take long for me to start dissecting the circumstances, shelving all the consequences. Bobby was distracting as a solar eclipse.

Mom turned left off Belmont and accelerated up Maple Avenue. The car made a loud clanking sound and then started vibrating weirdly. The engine slowly drained of power.

"I can't believe this." Mom pounded the steering wheel, then leaned forward, trying to motivate it farther.

"What is it?" I asked.

The car sputtered to a stop and died a humble death in the right lane of Maple Avenue. Mom got out first and I gradually followed. She found the latch behind the grill and opened the hood. Oil was splattered everywhere.

"Oh no." Mom leaned away from it, shook her head, held one hand to her mouth. A slight wisp of smoke rose from somewhere below the maze of dirty hoses. It smelled like something was burning.

"Do you think it might explode?" I asked.

"I don't think it'll do anything." Mom dropped the hood. She looked real disappointed, and I know it had nothing to do with the car. She looked up the road, as if maybe we'd walk there, then looked back the other way, as if we might hitch-hike, then looked over at me.

"I'll walk back to the intersection and call a tow truck. You stay here."

I got back in the car and watched Mom in the rearview

mirror headed back the other way. Her head was slung down
like some used-up whore on the way home from a long night's
labor. She had the worst of luck but only blamed herself. I
really loved her because she never took it out on me.

A big blue sedan stopped beside her. Mom leaned into the
passenger window, then got into the car, and I'm thinking, *She
is such a catch*. The car rolled up and damn if it wasn't the
astronaut. Mom waved me over, but something was holding
me back, some incredible weight was in my lap and I couldn't
budge. Mom rolled down her window, waved again, this time
more vigorously.

"Dan will give us a lift," she called out. "We can call a tow
truck from the church!" Mom smiled and waved again.

I leaned against the door with all my weight and knocked it
open, then made my way over to the other one, a little wobbly
in heels. Mom opened her door, scooted over, and patted the
seat.

"Isn't this the most amazing coincidence?" she asked.

"Divine intervention," Dan said. "The work of the Lord."
And I almost think he believed it. I slammed the door, looked
into the side mirror, and watched the Ford getting smaller and
smaller, realizing I was saying good-bye to my old life and hello
to my new one.

Mom seemed to absorb the incident like a horoscope that
comes true. Dan had a wide slippery grin leaking all over his
face like he'd just won the trifecta and all his years of gambling
had finally paid off.

We veered into the church driveway and the astronaut
dropped Mom and I at the door, then circled around the big
crowded lot and parked the car. I followed Mom, hesitantly,

into the church. We hung up our coats in the community closet, then Mom went to the pay phone and made arrangements with AAA. I made a visit to the ladies' room. One good thing about Lutherans is they're tidy, a side effect of that watered-down Germanic heritage: Cleanliness is next to godliness and all that crap. The toilet paper was crisp as sandpaper, as if God wanted you to suffer even in here. I slapped on a fresh layer of lip gloss and blended back into the crowd.

A shiny transparency clung to every surface, the stained-glass windows burst to life in the morning sunlight. The music started pumping up the crowd. Trying to remain inconspicuous, I browsed the literature. The organ fund-raiser thermometer was halfway to the top, the bulletin board had the softball schedule with the home games highlighted. In the lobby there was a painting of Jesus with blond hair and blue eyes, as if he were Swedish or something.

The astronaut came in and greeted all the regulars. The church was full of women marked with studied makeup and slouching men in ill-fitting suits. He took my mother's arm and led us toward our seats. Walking up the center aisle I got the feeling this was a test drive, that Mom was tumbling forward into marriage with the velocity of a bowling ball rolling toward the pins. We sat in the fourth row and I immediately broke into a cold sweat, got conscious of my body odor, felt a million eyeballs burning into the back of my head. It seemed like the whole world was whispering and I was on the wrong end of the story.

I wondered if the mechanic was dreaming of me, whether he'd call me this afternoon, whether or not our lives would

come crashing together. Finally I had a reason to pray. I bowed
my head and tried to focus, but had the feeling the line was
busy.

A wooden crucifix hung above the altar, the arms fully extended, the feet nailed into the wood. It seemed so hardcore.
The first hymn started and the crowd rose to its feet as a
procession marched up the center aisle: first an altar boy carry-
ing a large ornate cross; followed by the second in command
wearing a long red silk scarf, then the big guy in a white and
gold motif, singing slightly off-key, a blue hymnal resting in
the palms of his hands, a large silver cross dangling over the
slope of his belly. I looked over at Mom. One hand was holding
a hymnal, the other clutching the pew in front of us. That's
when I noticed she was wearing her new ring. The diamond
looked even bigger than yesterday, as if it had mushroomed
overnight.

The organist whipped through chorus after chorus, the congregation moaned through the words. Afterward the pastor
stood and motioned us all to sit down, which was good because
my feet were killing me. He burned through the first dose of
liturgy. There was another song, a few more prayers, some
chanting, and then everyone settled in for the sermon. A few
sporadic coughs echoed from the back of the room, people
shifted in their seats, trying to find a comfortable position in
the wood pews. And then a dopey silence minced the room as
the old man flipped on the reading light of his pulpit.

"My friends," he started. "We are in a time of unparalleled
change. A time when tomorrow looks nothing like yesterday.
But, my friends, one thing never changes! The love of Jesus.
Amen."

The minister's message was a classic doom-and-gloom end-of-the-world paranoia speech. He used the petrochemical fire as a stage for all his wigged-out ideas. I looked over at Mom. The words washed over her like frosting. She was gazing high above the altar. Her thoughts were far beyond this room.

I wondered if heaven—being the opposite of hell—was a cold place, a golden city aloft in frosty clouds complete with idyllic suburbs and snow piled along the driveways? If heaven were a perfect place then would there be snow? Is snow good or evil?

When the sermon ended the minister turned off the spotlight on his pulpit. The congregation flipped open their hymnals and shuffled through the pages. The organist stumbled through the melody once so everyone could get their shit together. It was another somber monotone number, something about lambs and shepherds and whatever.

The tax collectors came by, holding large gold dishes filled with discreet white envelopes and folded dollar bills, then came the body and blood thing, which just totally gives me the creeps. Everyone paraded down the center aisle like zombies. People knelt at the altar twelve at a time eating the body of Christ, then drinking his blood! It was so satanic. If I were in a heavy metal band this would be my video. Jesus could've been an awesome rock star.

The ceremony finally ended with one last rousing number about marching off to war, then everyone began to file out. I was totally relieved. After the service I was called into duty and shook hands with the minister and a few trustees, then got my coat and went outside. The morning sky was full of tears, a steady baptism that cleansed my soul of that pornography of suffering. How anybody could think that God had any connection to some compound off Route 53 in Lisle is beyond me, but what worried me more was how many more there were just like it. Sometimes I worry that God was like an essence that's been all used up. Mom and I stood under an umbrella while Dan brought the car around.

"The last time I was in church I got married," Mom said.

"Well one for two isn't bad," I said.

Dan drove us to the gas station. The windshield wipers flapped back and forth, re-creating the same monotonous feeling rambling through my heart. Black clouds muddied the sky a feverish black and blue. It looked like tornado weather. Mr. Astronaut turned on his headlights as a precaution. I flashed back through all my Sunday school stories: the woman who turned into salt, Noah's ark, Adam and Eve, the burning bush, the star in the East. There was a lot of weird shit going down back then.

Rain began to fall as we pulled into the gas station. Dan parked the car, and we all got out. I felt myself retracing steps from the night before: the Coke machine; the cigarette butts on the floor. I could tell by the sad look in the eyes of the tow truck driver that our beater was dead.

"You could fix it," he said, "but the investment would probably cost more than what you paid for it." The astronaut peeked under the hood. "Needs a ring job."

I ran my hand over the Ford's cold dented fender. The chipped paint was rusting in the corners, the milky windshield cracked, the tires bald, the upholstery was ripped and shedding its yellow foam. The car was a suitcase of childhood memories. The interior smelled as familiar as my bedroom. I opened the

back door and lifted the seat for loose change, found a button
off my army jacket, remembered struggling out of it one par-
ticularly frustrating night when my boyfriend of the moment,
Tommy Mulligan, came so fast his love lasted the duration of
a drive-thru. I checked under the floor mats, grabbed the maps
and the windshield scraper out of the glove box. Mom popped
the trunk, but all she salvaged was a tire iron and a half empty
bottle of windshield washer fluid.

"Is Bobby working tonight?" I asked the attendant.

"Sheriff just came by asking the same question," he said,
rubbing his chin.

"What do you mean?"

"Someone saw the tow truck lifting a car out of the Meadowbrook Mall last night." His right eye kept flinching. "Only
one person drives that truck. I don't know what he would've
done with it." He looked at me sorta suspicious, as if maybe it
was stashed over at my house.

"You a friend of his?" he asked.

"Not really." I looked away from his nosy eyes, turned and
walked back toward the astronaut's car. The old man knew I
was lying. I could feel him watching my every step.

On the way home the car's silence held the weight of a
funeral. Mom had lost her car and I had probably lost my mechanic. Bobby lied to me. He told me he was going to clear
the highway when actually he went to sweep a parking lot.

"Who's Bobby?" Mom asked.

"Just some guy," I said.

Mom was too distracted by her current affairs to risk falling
into mine, especially in front of the astronaut. She slipped into
one of her spacey interludes, locking into another conversation

tuned in from the spiritual world of her fuzzy mind. "How will I buy groceries and get to work?" she asked out loud.

Dan cleared his throat, seized the opportunity, and offered up his ex-wife's car. "It's just getting dusty in the garage," he insisted. "Go on, take it. Please?"

Mom hesitated for about a second, looking over at me for reassurance. "Really?" her voice dropped an octave, like she was drunk or insincere. Maybe she was in shock. I really don't know. Dan was beaming like a victorious politician on election night.

It was definitely the moment she threw her life into his. Suddenly tangled by insurance forms and mutual signatures, her life would now be supported, assisted, and watched over by a man. She knew the car was more than a gesture. It was the beginning. First the ring, now the car, how much more did she need to realize that her life would be much easier in marriage, that she'd have the things she needed, that she wouldn't have to worry anymore? I could see her tired eyes smiling with a mixture of hope and relief: hope that it will turn out all right and relief that the ambulance came so soon.

THE MALL

HEN I opened the door the phone was ringing. It was Tracy, drooling for details about last night. Who kissed who? How many times? Dadadadadada. Finally, she just hung up, got in her car, and rushed over.

Tracy wanted to check out some nose hardware at the mall. Mom wanted to come too, but I eighty-sixed her. I changed into some baggy jeans and my Cat in the Hat T-shirt, then laced up my Romper Stompers. Tracy showed up in a sheer white nightgown layered over a vintage white slip, dark purple lipstick, and matching eye shadow, à la *Night of the Living Dead*. Tracy was going through a mild Goth phase. She wanted to be an artist, even if it just meant decorating herself.

Tracy and I have become social outcasts at school. We distanced ourselves from the normals, tried to make a new scene, but didn't necessarily acquire any followers. I guess you could say we're stuck up, but for obvious reasons.

The mall was our own private biosphere. We spent hours combing magazines at Barnes & Noble—analyzing fashion trends, pouring over horoscopes, and drooling over rock stars. Tracy and I could sit in Starbuck's for hours going over every detail of our latest encounters or infatuations, scrutinizing the possibilities down to the most minuscule proportions.

"So how did he do it?" Tracy reached in her bag for a cigarette with one hand, balanced the wheel of the car with the other.

"Do what?" I turned the other way.

"Make the first move," she asked. And then before I could answer, "Did you go all the way?"

"My mom's getting married."

"Don't change the subject."

"I'm serious! She's gonna marry the astronaut."

"So what? She's been married before."

"That was before I was born. I'm being inherited by a stranger."

"Your mom trusts him, why shouldn't you?"

"I'm not as desperate."

"Oh yeah? Tell me what happened last night. I deserve chronological order."

"Well." I hesitated a few seconds, watched Tracy lean forward with anticipation. "The coolest thing is that he races a car at Santa Fe Speedway."

"No way."

"Can you believe it? I saw the car, it's orange and black. He told me his grandfather was a bootlegger and that his father died in the Vietnam War."

"What happened to his mother?" Tracy asked.

"I didn't get that far."

"How far did you get?"

"I'm trying to tell a story."

"Well, hurry up and get to the good part."

"We couldn't get a parking spot near the fire, so Bobby drove out to the woods near the quarry instead. We walked through the trees to a clearing overlooking the canal. He spread out a blanket and we started talking."

"Yeah, yeah . . ." She turned her hand over, motioning me to fast-forward.

"Then he made me close my eyes and fed me wild raspberries."

"He what?"

"It kind of grossed me out at first. I thought it was an eyeball or something."

"So then what happened?"

"Major horizontal action." I smiled.

"Oh my God!" Tracy overdramatized each word. "You made out with him on the first date?"

"You always make out on the first date!"

"I would have put up a little struggle," Tracy said, looking the other way, "at least tried to tag him out sliding into second or something. I thought this was going to be a long-term relationship?"

"I was all worked up. He smelled like dirty motor oil. My hormones were under full-scale attack."

"Earth to Chrissie!" Tracy yelled. "Hello!"

"I tried slowing things down. I even told him I was having my period." I tried to sound convincing.

"What did he say?"

"He said he was having his exclamation point."

Tracy cracked up. "So how did you stop him?" She pillaged her tape case, found her Riot Grrl compilation, cranked up L7.

"Stop him what?"

"You know, from a home run on opening day."

"He stopped himself. I was looking for a condom in my purse when his beeper went off. He told me it meant there was an accident on the highway, but I found out this morning he used the tow truck to steal a car out of the Meadowbrook parking lot."

"What?"

"Mom's car broke down on the way to church and it was towed to the gas station. When I asked if Bobby was working tonight the guy said the cops had already been there this morning asking the same question."

"Why would he steal a car? He already has two."

"I think his friends needed parts for the car. He told me this whole story about his past, now I wonder if any of it was true."

"Do you suppose he's fired?" Tracy asked.

"He might be in jail."

Tracy rummaged for a cigarette, working her pockets with increasing speed. She found an empty package, threw it in the backseat.

"What's your mood ring say?" Tracy asked.

I held the ring up to the light. "Blue and white," I said.

"What's blue and white mean?"

"Moody, I guess."

We rolled down the hill past the glass-box office buildings snugging the interstate. There were no names on the buildings, no identifying colors.

"Look!" Tracy pointed. Somebody had spray-painted on the Village of Lombard sign, HOME OF THE UNABOMBER.

THE INFIRMARY

MY locker is on the third floor, which is a drag. There's nothing worse than StairMaster first thing in the morning. We're not allowed to decorate them on the outside, but on the inside it's makeover city. Mine is plastered with pictures torn from magazines of boys whose names I'll never know and whose faces I'll never meet. My music shrine is currently dedicated to Françoise Hardy. She's a French pop star from the sixties. I got hooked after buying a couple of CDs at Jewel's garage sale. How he came across them was a long sordid story involving an Air France pilot that I will not repeat here.

Anyway, the infirmary has been bustling with graduation fever. Today we cast our ballots for king and queen of the last dance. What a sorry lot of choices. Everyone is matching up for the final party, signing yearbooks with promises to get in touch over the summer. As anxious as I am for it to end, I can sense a certain loss, like a distant relative dying. I'll have to ask myself some fun questions like "What am I going to do with my life?" and spend hours in front of the mirror repeating "I'm not a loser. I'm not a loser." My grandma wants me to go to college, but I just dread the idea of more school. What else is there to know?

My counselor suggested that if I want to be a filmmaker I should get a job at a video store. "If you want to be a writer," he said, "try a bookstore."

"What if I want to be a supermodel?" I asked.

"Well, you've certainly got the attitude." He stood to let me know our session was over. "Don't be afraid of life's challenges," he said, patting me on the back, then waved in the next student.

I went to the library, opened my social studies book, and stared at the same paragraph for an hour. The room smelled like static electricity, the only noise came from the hum of microfiche and Xerox machines. The library was unusually crowded, a side effect of last-minute cramming. I thought I had it bad, but the girl across from me was obviously going through a serious mental breakdown. Her skin had a feverish purple tint and she was breaking out all over the place. She had that hollowed eyed "I've been studying for two hundred hours" face, when somebody is trying to cram a whole year's worth of education into the last twenty minutes. Wearing black on black on black, her orange hair was teased with a couple gallons of hairspray so that she looked like a living troll doll. She was possessed by a book called *In Cold Blood*, probably picking up a few pointers.

My boat was sinking just as quickly. I have to turn in an

economics report on downsizing tomorrow that's totally depressing because, when all is said and done, downsizing basically means we'll end up doing our parents' jobs at half the wages. In some ways it seems like the more intelligent I get the more aware I become of my own inherited doom. I glanced over the next paragraph, then flipped through a few more pages, looking for a chart or a photograph to ease my pain. My eyes were beyond tired.

Sometimes school just seems like a way to keep our minds off television, a little bit of vegetables in a world of brain candy. Other times it felt like a discipline compound, a place to be brainwashed and homogenized, where everyone learned to be just like everyone else. I wonder what it's done to me and how many years it will take to shed all this skin. I wonder if I could sue for damages.

SIN CITY

WHEN I got home Mom was in the kitchen sporting some slinky black dress, black nylons, and some extra-high heels. A couple pieces of luggage were stacked beside the door.

"Where are you going?" I set my books at the bottom of the staircase.

"Honey." She posed in front of the hall mirror while adjusting an earring. "Dan has some business in Las Vegas and he asked me to come along."

"What kind of business?"

"Oh you know, religious stuff."

"Since when does God hang out in Vegas?"

"I'll be back on Monday. No parties! Do you hear me young lady?" She acted all authoritarianlike and everything. "I left some money and the number for the Stardust Hotel beside the phone. There's spaghetti sauce thawing in the fridge." She kissed me on the cheek and then scribbled on another layer of lipstick. Dan pulled into the driveway. I heard the car door slam, then the doorbell rang.

Mom opened the door. "You're late," she said. Dan kissed her. Her shoulders caved and she let out a crazy giggle and gently pushed him away. "Stop it," she said.

"Hi, Chrissie." He waved at me all innocent, like he was Tom Sawyer taking Becky for a peek in the caves. The astronaut took my mother's bags and locked them in the trunk, then swung around the car and opened the door for her.

"You keep an eye on your brother," Mom said, pointing at me, then leaned into the car. Dan closed Mom's door then pranced over to his.

Standing at the window was like watching a movie of my own life ending, the cameras still rolling. Mom waved at me from behind the windshield and I waved back at her. The car slid out of the driveway and curled up the cul-de-sac. My stomach was queasy. I went into the kitchen and poured myself a Diet Coke.

The basement door cracked open and the troll popped out of his crypt. "How are we supoosed to get food?" my brother asked, standing in the stairwell, wrapped in his musty bathrobe, suddenly paranoid about his dwindling frozen waffle supply.

"You'll just have to learn how to use the microwave all by yourself," I said. "Don't you think there are a few slightly larger issues here?"

"What? Are we out of frozen pizza?"

"You're about to be adopted!"

David waddled into the kitchen like a hundred-year-old man and opened the freezer. "I don't know what you're getting so worked up about, that guy is about as dangerous as a couch."

"I think they're going to Vegas to get hitched."

"Well then, we should celebrate." He shut the freezer door and opened the refrigerator.

"That's it?"

"You got any better ideas?"

DEATH PRINCESS

I went upstairs and lay down on my bed. If I had a dollar for every minute spent staring out my dirty window scribbling wandering poems about misplaced feelings and aborted love I'd be as rich as Madonna, but I never thought I'd be draining ink from my pen worrying about my mother.

It's weird when your mom's trial and error starts to overshadow your own. The astronaut has shuttled her off to sin city with the intention of a final seduction. The man is in high gear, whipping out his finest polyester, working all the night moves. Mom is defenseless. She's a suitcase looking for a vacation, and so she swims into the dark corners of DuPage County and surfaces with Captain Kirk, right-wing lover boy, used-car dealer, man of God. He's a step back in her evolution. She's sacrificing big-time. Mom needs to get out more, but I can't be the cruise director fishing for a dreamboat. Her decision to get married has really put a snag in my tights. I know

I should be happy for her and feel all that "if she's happy, then I'm happy" stuff, but it's not working. I can't find the light switch.

My brother is about as helpful as Mr. Potato Head. He'll spend the rest of his life baking in front of the boob tube, shrugging me off with enlightened arrogance, as if there were any accomplishment to swallowing pills that spin your eyeballs in circles. David's locked into a superslack depression cycle. Like a giant vacuum cleaner, he sucks all the air out of the room. His obsession with death has been flourishing. His wardrobe has been reduced to black pajamas. He's taken up clove cigarettes and likes to disappear on long walks through the cemetery where he traces etchings from tombstones. One wall of his room is covered with them. He also bought a bug light a few months ago, hung it on the porch, and started a collection of moths zapped by his purple ring of fire. Their beautiful wings harden into stiff weightless specimens. He spends hours building meticulous wood cases in my father's workshop to exhibit their frozen eternal beauty. The moths are pinned side by side with their Latin names typed onto small strips of white paper and glued to a purple velvet lining. It's one of the few occupations he seems to enjoy, as if maybe he were studying to be a taxidermist or an undertaker or a serial killer or something. He's getting weirder by the minute. But maybe I'm just projecting my own cloud upon him. He could be perfectly normal for all I know.

My death princess hours are usually spent in the willow tree playing with the puppetry of danger, but last night I rode my bike through Denburn Woods and sat beside the Burlington Northern tracks. The greasy scent of railroad ties smelled like ancient history. The tracks looked like an old scar sewing up some forgotten wound. I watched a freight train rumble through town. Its tall rattling cars were rusting; beside the faded serial numbers were exotic names like Pacific and Chesapeake. Some steel doors were open and I could see shadowy figures hunched in the moonlight, hobos or homeless people headed for the next stop or the one after that. It was one of those nights when I wanted to either jump the train or put my head on the tracks, but didn't have the courage to do either one.

Outside the window, beyond the trees, the thick black plume of the Lemont Fire billowed into the heavens like a mushroom cloud, then tilted and dissipated into the upper atmosphere. I wondered if the atmosphere was like an old dishwasher, and whether after a while the glasses would start coming out spotted.

On Earth Day a scientist from Argonne National Laboratory came to our school and told us toxicology was one of the fastest growing fields in the scientific community. Sometimes I dream of being a forest ranger, someone who tracks bears and repairs trails and points in the right direction when befuddled tourists find themselves lost at a trailhead, but something tells me I'm going to end up a cashier at Taco Bell or working the Slurpee machine at 7-Eleven for snotty teenagers raised on *Beavis & Butt-head*. My greatest fear is to be known as the girl with the purple hair that works at Barnes & Noble.

Tracy says we should move into the city after graduation and get an apartment in Wicker Park because a lot of cool bands live there. She thinks we should start our own band and become famous rock stars with lunch boxes full of money to buy frilly dresses and fingernail polish.

But that dream reeks of some hole-in-the-wall apartment and a menial job that provides a check just barely big enough to blow on potato chips and beer. Tracy wants me to work at a copyshop so I can make free posters. I told her working in a bookstore would make me a better lyricist, then we got into a huge fight over who would write the songs, even though neither one of us can play a single chord on the guitar yet.

7 - ELEVEN

I F you're going to have a party, life begins at 7-Eleven, the front line of civilization, the glass doors to convenience, the place most likely to accept my fake ID. Tracy bounced into the parking lot and nearly made a hood ornament out of a pair of skaters jumping over empty beer cans. She swayed to the right and parked beside the Dumpster, as far away as possible from the front door. David handed me a twenty. "Think quantity, not quality," he said, leaning up to let me out of the backseat.

The skaters were dressed like scarecrows: big baggy pants, baby dread hair, and golf caps turned around backward. Their boom box was blasting the new Beastie Boys record. A pair of waifish tomboy groupies stood next to the yellow plastic garbage can with hands planted deep in their front pockets. They looked like a couple of totem poles. A red sign in the window said WE DON'T SERVE SKATERS.

The tallest one jumped off the parking curb, did a curlicue pattern on his board, and followed me up to the door. His hair was dyed Gatorade green, his skin already pockmarked by years of french fries and Pepsi. His eyes had a crazy intensity that made him if not sexy at least alluring.

"Say a . . . miss, can you do me a favor?" He rolled closer, waved a five spot with his right hand. "I lost my ID and my dog just got run over by a car and my dad, he's got Alzheimer's disease 'cause he swears I'm not his son, and well, my friends and I, we've come across a wave of hostility from the management of this corporate money-laundering facility." He pointed at the sign in the window. "Would you mind picking up a few quarts for me and my brothers," he said, nodding back toward his crew. They looked as gangly and dysfunctional as their leader, rocking out to the skanky noise booming from their blaster.

"You can keep the change," he said, as if to jelly my toasting decision.

I took his five dollars, opened the glass door and headed for the beer cooler, grabbed a twelve-pack of Old Style for us and two quarts of Schlitz Malt Liquor for satan's children, then dragged it all up to the counter. The cashier was some aging hottie.

"Weren't you in my math class?" I tried flirting to avoid the ID mess altogether. His face scrunched up, and I saw him paging his memory bank, trying to come up with a matching face from his glorious past. It usually works. He gave me a second look while ringing up the beer.

"That's sixteen thirty-seven," he said. "You got an ID?" I

handed him a twenty tucked around my card. He looked at the name, sifted his registry, passed it back. "You must be thinking of someone else." He sorta puffed up his chest, as if that other guy I was thinking about was Arnold Schwarzenegger or something. He looked marinated in gloom, as if he was just biding time, waiting for the big tornado to put an end to his misery.

"I hated math." He dipped his fingers into the till, dished out my change.

"Me too." I stared at the purple stain on his orange smock, grabbed the bag, and walked out the door. The skaters circled me like a bunch of blood-hungry vampires.

"Don't try and rip us off, lady," my romeo skatepunk said, whirling toward me.

I set their beers beside the garbage can. "Here ya go, sweetie." I smiled. "Call me when you get a bigger chariot." The beer rats jumped on the bag. I scooted out of the way, stepped off the ledge. My brother opened the car door, lifted his seat. He was curled over the dashboard with his ear pinned to the car speaker, trying to tune in some obscure Fox River pirate radio. I squeezed into the backseat. Tracy backed out and spun around the corner, mission accomplished.

For some reason Tracy was being unusually quiet, as if she were trying to emulate my brother's lack of communication with the outside world, like maybe he would notice her if she too were invisible, someone who made no effort to scrape his fragile surroundings. She obviously saw the DO NOT DISTURB billboard pasted to his pimple-scarred forehead.

"Earth to David," I said. "Come in David."

He didn't respond, fixated with the control knob of the radio, listening for a faint signal in the white noise.

"Yo, dj!" I slapped him on the back of the head.

"What?" he asked, still working the radio dial.

"Why do you take drugs?"

"To distract me from my boredom."

"Are you bored now?" I asked.

"Yes."

"What can we do to make your life more interesting?"

"Take drugs."

"I see. Are you suicidal?"

"Maybe."

"I can't believe anyone would kill themselves over a concept."

"It's a condition."

"So turn on the air conditioner."

"There's a gadget for every weakness, isn't there?" he asked.

"You're the one controlling the dial."

"What are you two talking about?" Tracy asked.

My brother leaned toward Tracy. "The airwaves are full of static," he said.

Tracy nodded, as if she understood what he meant.

David turned and looked at me. "Can I get off the couch now?" he asked.

"Sorry," I said. "I just wanted to poke around the fire a bit."

"And your conclusion, Doctor?"

"There's plenty of kindling."

THE PARTY

MOM blasts off with the astronaut so Mister Antisocial comes out of the cellar and decides, under the guided peer pressure of his morbid friends, to have a little get-together to celebrate his dubious accomplishments. Tracy, the social butterfly, has already announced it to half the universe, and I'm instantly Miss Popular at school. When I sat down in the cafeteria I was circled by the dogs of night, a group of degenerate snobs looking for a place to park their boyfriends. I gave them a bogus address, but that just added to the hysteria. I've become the flavor of the minute and was even picked for the best volleyball team in gym class.

Tracy drags me shopping, not once, but twice, for the elusive outfit that will capture the zeitgeist and slay my brother into submission. She thinks that given the opportunity she can snag him into a luscious make-out session that will prove so distracting he'll forget his entire past, wrap around the moment, and consume her until kingdom come. I told her all she had to do was just scrape up a few bong hits and buy a twelve-pack of Ding Dongs and she'd be *In Like Flint*, but Tracy has a mind of her own.

She was wearing a white miniskirt and a skintight baby tee with a small red heart pasted in the center, pink sparkle tights, and white Mary Janes. She looked like a scoop of vanilla ice cream with a cherry on top, which I presume is exactly the comparison she was looking for.

The teenager formerly known as David has decided to jam with some friends at the party, so they've been holed up in the basement night and day practicing three-chord moshes. The noise and repetition were unbearable, but the drummer was kind of cute.

This whole party thing was completely the wrong direction, it's so last year. I'm trying to project myself out of high school, far away from all the riffraff. I don't want to be the fairy god-mother of puking teenagers who lost their car keys. I'm doing this for Tracy, and my brother, who seems strangely motivated by the potential for anarchy. The introvert will finally have a chance to interact with his public.

Tracy will park herself in front of the band and dance like a maniac until my brother looks up from his guitar strings long enough to discover he has groupies. I put her in charge of the backyard decor, so she strung multicolored tiki lights through the tree branches and stuck lawn torches in the grass around the perimeter.

"I want it to look like someone is going to sacrifice a virgin," she said.

I did a house check, concealed anything remotely valuable, tied the can opener to the refrigerator door, made more ice, found another roll of paper towels in the cabinet. I opened a few more windows and took the fan out of the closet. David and his friends were doing bong hits in the garage, finalizing their set list. I loved David, but his music was a bit harsh.

"What do we do if the quarterback shows up with last year's football heroes?" I asked.

"Would you get over that," Tracy barked. "Those losers wouldn't dare fuck with us because they know we're not afraid to fuck with them."

"We're not?"

"No, we're not."

The first people arrived around 9 P.M. and it was like a trout stream steadily thereafter. I stood at the door for a while but hardly recognized anyone. There were a lot of people from last year and the year before that, all my brother's underworld friends. It wasn't long before the backyard was full of slouching nobodies toting twelve-packs. David's bug zapper kept a crowd of stoners entertained. They stood in silent reverence for hours watching insects get toasted.

The party went its usual course. We were out of beer in about ten seconds. Cars lined the cul-de-sac, the house filled up with smoke, someone broke a glass in the kitchen, and then David's band kicked in and the house shook like a truck driving over a rickety bridge. It took one phone call from an irate neighbor and there were instantly men in blue uniforms on the front porch peering through the window. Word spread through the crowd like there was an Ebola outbreak. People slipped out through the sliding-glass doors and disappeared into The Field, doubling back to collect their cars. The cops were creeping around the yard with flashlights, probably planting evidence like they did to O.J.

David was buried in the mobbed basement experimenting with deafening feedback and distortion. Sergeant Drexler gave me about five seconds to find the fuse box and drain the juice on David's petri dish and send all the rejects home to the safety of their parents' absent love. I smiled ear to ear and played the honor roll student, blamed the noise on the delinquency of today's youth and the lack of alternatives, i.e., a recreation hall where teenagers could mingle on Friday nights under the guidance of supervisors and sip punch and talk about conservative issues, like more cops and more jails. But then Drexler told me to shut up or I'd be spending the night in one, so I did, but only as a silent protest. I knew my rights and nobody had read them to me. Once the music was off, the cops cooled down and suddenly seemed anxious to get back to their doughnuts, coffee, and radar patrol on the backroads of suburban nowheresville.

The party was over before it got started. We were lucky nothing got wasted, considering how many empties were left behind. Tracy and I settled in the living room listening to one of my dad's old Astrud Gilberto records. We were both pretty wasted. David burst into the room and accused Tracy of inviting too many people.

"I did not!"

"You did so!"

And so on.

Some of David's friends made themselves at home and eventually crashed wherever they got comfortable. Tracy waited up half the night but never got the invitation she was hoping for. I found her in my bed sound asleep still wearing her white Mary Janes.

LAS   VEGAS   REDUX

THE next day I awoke with a vicious hangover and a severe dose of paranoia. Mom was coming home, which meant, among other things, that she was married, broke, or maybe both. Vegas was one of those towns in the back of my mind that flickered like an all-night movie. A dreamy world of lights and sensuality, of passion and heartbreak, a place where men are gangsters, women are whores, and the drinks are free.

Mom got out of the taxi wearing sunglasses as big as pancakes, looking like Jackie O. the morning after. She darted for the door as if she were weary about cul-de-sac headlines. I heard the key fit into the slot and the door suck open. Mom dropped her bags at the foot of the stairs. I had a feeling there was trouble. She came home at a strange time and in a strange car. Her footsteps into the kitchen did not hold the weight of true love and happiness. The refrigerator opened and closed. She shuffled through the mail.

"Is anybody home?" she yelled.

I didn't answer her. The house was quiet as a spider's web. The wind rattled the windows, and it looked like there was some serious rain charging out of the west. I wasn't very interested in dealing with one of her moods but felt hopelessly drawn by a scorching curiosity about her weekend, so finally I went downstairs to find out what happened.

Mom was outside picking up pears out of the yard. I could hear them plopping into the bucket. Each thump made me feel a little more uneasy. The trees were so old they shed fruit all year long. The pears weren't edible unless you were a squirrel. Mom used them for her compost. I couldn't tell whether she was working out aggression or just stretching after a long flight.

I opened the screen door. "Welcome back!" I shouted. I could tell a mile away Mom was upset. Her moods were as subtle as a car alarm.

"Need some help?" I asked.

"Sure." She tossed me an empty bucket. "Did you guys have a party while I was gone?" She immediately put me on the defensive.

"Of course not," I said. "Why?"

"I found beer bottles in two different places, the grass is matted down, there are cigarette butts everywhere. What was going on here? Woodstock?"

"Must have been those rotten little kids down the street. How was Vegas?"

"All right." She sounded suspicious.

"Was the hotel nice?"

"It was fine."

"Did you win any money?"

"Not really."

"And the drinks were free?"

"Depends on your point of view."

"Did you get married?"

"Dan took me to a party and turned into Hugh Hefner. He got it in his head that the bunnies were interchangeable." Mom threw her hair back away from her face, as if she were swatting it all away. "I took a taxi to the airport and left on the next plane."

"You just left him there?"

"The man got so drunk he fell in the pool." She bent over and picked up another pear, dropped it into the bucket. "I should have never gotten mixed up with him. He's got some serious problems. I went through all this with your father. I'm not interested in reruns." Mom reached down, picked up a pear, and dropped it into the bucket.

"Men are about as predictable as the weather," I said. "One minute they love you and the next minute you're in the way."

"Wait a minute." She leaned up. "Since when do you start consoling me about men? Don't you have any homework?"

"I always have homework."

"Then you should be upstairs studying."

"I'm taking a little break."

Mom picked up some more pears. I could almost hear the arguments going on in her head. She seemed more frustrated than angry, as if she had lost the marathon after training for years and years.

"So what are we going to do for your graduation? Should we have a party or did you already take care of that?" She picked up a cigarette butt, flicked it into the pail, then sat on the rocks outlining the garden. "Sit down." She patted a rock beside her. "I want to discuss something with you."

I took a seat and prepared for the worst.

"First of all. I want you to know how proud I am that you're graduating from high school. I know we've had some disagreements on our way to the finish line, I just hope you won't hold them against me, okay? I've always wanted what's best for you kids, but sometimes I slip up. I just hope you learn from my mistakes. Have you heard from any colleges yet?"

"A few," I lied.

"I hope you get in. Stay around here and you'll end up like all the other mailboxes. Soon the highlight of your day will be scanning the newspaper for coupons."

"You've never clipped a coupon in your life," I said.

"All right, so maybe I'm a bad example, but you know what I mean."

SMOKE

DOOMSDAY strikes. Finals. The algebra test. With the added luck of multiple choice and the fact that we are being graded on the curve, I should definitely be able to slip by with a C or a D. The classroom was hushed in all-out brain fever. You could smell the synapses burning. I stared out the window, trying to remember the formulas of several equations—which seemed to be tangled together or linked backward or forward or worse—when all of a sudden the fire alarm sounded and a big cheer resounded through the hallways.

"Turn in your test unfinished!" Ms. Carson yelled.

I jumped up and set my test on the front desk, then hurried out of the classroom before anyone changed their mind. I couldn't wait to get outside and have a smoke. The weird thing is I could kinda smell smoke in the hallway, and I wondered, could this be for real?

The stairwell was packed and some rowdy boys were trying

to exascerbate the hysteria. I went outside and parked on the lawn, watching the fire trucks roll in one after another, their sirens wailing full tilt like it was the Towering Inferno or something. It was so beautiful outside I wanted to kiss whoever pulled the alarm and saved me from that mind-frying torture. I lit a cigarette and leafed through my math book, looked up some formulas for the algebra questions, then scribbled them on my wrist with a black pen. Math sucks. Trigonometry should be left to specialists. Why does everybody have to learn the formula that makes triangles? Unless you're planning on doing something totally irrational like riding on the space shuttle, there was very little need for big math.

We got beached in the grass for half an hour because apparently there was a small fire somewhere in the building. When the firemen retreated and the student body was finally allowed to return to their classrooms, I got clipped from the crowd by Vice Principal O'Leary. He led me into his office for questioning. O'Leary was a big man. Intimidating. He smelled like military aftershave. His office was so anal, even the photos on his desk were in formation. It looked like some kind of interrogation room; there was a black vinyl chair and a small white rug, but no coffee table or magazines. The only other furniture was a lamp at the edge of his large black desk. It was like the biggest desk you've ever seen.

"Listen," I said. "I was taking a test, check it out, it wasn't me."

"Yes, but it was your locker. Tell me, who would do such a thing and why would they do it to you?" He looked the other way, as if to make it easier for me to confess.

"What do you mean?" I was mortified, started sweating,

trying to remember what was in my locker, wondering if there was anything in there that shouldn't have been.

"The fire started in your locker." He shrugged his shoulders. "Did you light your books on fire as some sort of practical joke?"

"I told you I was in math class taking a test," I said.

"Maybe you had a timer device?" He leaned over the desk.

"What am I? The Unabomber?"

"That's what I'm trying to find out," he said.

"Ever heard of random violence?" I kept my cards close to my chest. O'Leary was anxious to hang this incident on my neck.

"Young lady, you are in very serious trouble. We are talking about the destruction of government property."

"I didn't do it!"

"I'm asking you who did!"

"How should I know?"

"Disgruntled boyfriend perhaps?"

"I wish."

"Then who?"

I knew a thousand who's but wasn't exactly sure which one. "You're the detective," I said. "You tell me."

"Don't get smart with me, young lady! I'm going to get to the bottom of this."

"Can I see my locker?" I asked.

"Yes, of course. We'll walk up there together." He led me toward the door. The receptionist stared at me like I was Charles Manson or something.

There was a small circle of gawkers pointing at me as I arrived with escort at the crime scene. My locker was history.

It's amazing what a shot glass of gasoline and a match will do to four years' worth of memorabilia. Everything was reduced to one soggy smelly *blech*, because what the fire didn't destroy, the firemen did. The door was only hanging by a single hinge, everything else was spilled onto the floor.

"Why was there a car battery in your locker?" he asked. "Were you trying to make a bomb?"

I didn't want to be connected to any car batteries. "It wasn't there this morning, sir. Those are my notes." I pointed to a bunch of charred papers. "Why would I do that?"

"I've heard every excuse imaginable from students trying to weasel their way through exams." He rubbed his forehead, then pointed at me. "If you fail your exams *you will* be back here next September." Mr. O'Leary turned and shuffled back to his office. "I can't help you unless you help me."

I pillaged through the wreckage. There wasn't anything I wanted anyway.

Tracy came running up with her camera. "Hold it right there," she said.

Flash. Flash. Flash.

LUNCHROOM

TRACY and I parked ourselves as far away as possible from everyone in the cafeteria. Strictly a playground of freshmen and sophomores, it was a good place to lay low. All the cool people usually drove to McDonald's or one of the other cowfrys. It just seemed like a good day to ground our usual flight.

"What if the world were to end today?" Tracy asked.

"Then all this would be meaningless. You're just looking for a way out of finals," I said.

Tracy unwrapped her peanut butter and jelly sandwich. I squirted some mustard on my veggieburger to give it a little flavor.

"Did you pass your history test?" I asked.

"I have to go to my teacher's office for some extra credit," she said.

I shot her a look.

"I'm just kidding." She rolled her eyes, acted unapologetic, as if she was sleeping with him anyway, and aren't I such a prude to have my nose so high in the air. "Any new clues as to who firebombed your locker?"

"What I want to know is how come I got torched and you didn't?"

"You obviously hang out with arsonists," she said. "Maybe the Magic geeks cast a spell on your locker, or maybe it was instantaneous combustion. I saw this special on *Mystery Theater* about it."

"This was not a divine event, Tracy." I sipped my milk carton. "You know exactly who would leave a car battery in my locker."

"It might have been somebody you don't even know: a sophomore with a crush and a few minor psychotic tendencies."

"It's a bad omen and you know it."

"Listen, it's finals, we're under a lot of stress, everyone is prone to be a little hysterical."

"I am not being hysterical!" I shouted.

"What about the curse?" Tracy asked.

"What about it?"

"Have you heard anything?"

"Can we please talk about something else?"

"Like what?"

"Like what we usually talk about. I don't care. Pick a topic. Men. Movies. Music. What about hair? We haven't talked about hair in a long time."

"Will you get real? God. You are so bent out of shape. It was just a prank, lighten up will ya? Or I won't share my good

news." Tracy dug around her purse until she pulled out a newspaper clipping and handed it to me. "Have you seen this?" It
was an article from the *Downers Grove Reporter* about the Miller
100. "Guess whose name is listed in the entries?"

"He's racing tonight?" I glanced over the article, scanning
for Bobby's name.

"I think it starts at eight."

"When can you pick me up?" I whispered.

"Excuse me?"

"Please," I begged.

"Well." She paused. "I'll have to take a shower and—"

"That could take hours."

"Or years if you don't shut up."

The buzzer rang and it was time to go take another final.

"I'm still grounded, so let's do a Patty Hearst at the mailbox
at seven. Okay?"

"Whatever you say, Tanya."

BAD VIBES

AFTER school I went home, laid on my bed, and tried to do some studying, but was too distracted by the day's events to concentrate, so I cleaned out my drawers and sifted through my memorabilia instead. Whenever I'm depressed I tend to spend hours trying to make sense of my life by putting it in some sort of chronological order. Organizing photographs in a time sequence helps me estimate whether I'm overdue for some climactic change like a broken leg or another doomed love affair. I found a picture of Mom when she was in high school during the sixties. She was doing a flower child number: miniskirt, beads, and rose-tinted glasses, wearing the same mysterious glare she does today. I wondered if Dad took the picture. Mom rarely talked about any of her other old boyfriends.

I looked out the window and saw her picking weeds out of the sprouting garden. I always wondered what Mom was

thinking when she was all alone. I wanted to be inside her head
and know everything about her, but it was impossible, because
I was me and she was she and after so many years the boundaries
were built to last forever. It's so weird that I'm old enough
now to feel both the pain of her struggle and the radical impulse
to avoid all her mistakes.

Mom was once a local beauty queen and did some regional
modeling, but apparently all that did was attract a lot of trial
and error, like my father. Dad was just back from Vietnam and
they swung through the boogie-fever seventies celebrating life
from the edge of a coke spoon. Their marriage was a dance
that ended just as confused as it began. Without a dowry or a
husband Mom charmed her way back into society using old
connections from her pageant days and quickly snagged some
part-time employment from the museum downtown. It's actually more like an old house stuffed with a bunch of junk
you're not allowed to touch. Mom says the dust is giving hell
to her allergies. Anyway, she bumped into the astronaut at one
of the museum's functions, and it's been ground control to
Major Dan ever since.

It makes me mad that Bobby didn't call and invite me to
the track. Sometimes I worry he's just like Dad and I'm about
to repeat all of my mother's errors. When I look into the mirror
I worry about the reflection, but I guess I have to make my
own mistakes. I just wish I'd taken better notes.

THE GETAWAY

A T seven o' clock I wandered outside and slowly made my way down the driveway. Inside the mailbox was a recruiting letter from the U.S. Army addressed to my brother. Mom usually leaves them on the stairs to the basement, thinking a green uniform might help him channel his adolescent anger, but he sends them back with all kinds of idiotic rantings like "Will I get to fire nuclear weapons on worthless third world countries?" When the local recruitier came to our school, David and his friends all wore dresses. It was a riot. They keep sending him more forms, so I guess he's just the kind of guy they're looking for.

I stuffed the envelope back into the box, sat on the curb, and picked weeds out of the grass, watching the corner, cursing Tracy's lateness. Some little kids were playing kick the can at the other end of the block, chasing one another around, screaming at the top of their lungs. Jewels was out spritzing his precious lawn in a white Speedo, pink thongs, and gold-rimmed glasses.

I picked a piece of clover out of the grass and pulled the leaves from its stem. "He loves me," I chanted, "he loves me not." Clover drives Jewels totally mad. He calls it Creeping Charley because it "spreads like communism." I pulled out a handful of proletarians, tore their heads off, tossed them onto the driveway to shrivel up and die.

I finally heard the Eurobeep and saw the kids scattering. Tracy's VW hurled down the winding cul-de-sac. She rolled up slowly and popped the door open like a kidnapper. I jumped inside and slammed the door. Tracy sped up the block, beeping again, swerving between the little monsters, who swore and made obscene gestures with their miniature hands. When we pulled out of the subdivision, I sat up, lit a cigarette, nervous about what I'd just done and the evening still ahead.

"I've never run away from home before," I said.

"Excuse me, but you're not running, you're riding." Tracy flipped her hair back. "I hope you have some gas money."

I took three dollars out of my pocket and slipped it into the ashtray.

"So how's it feel to be jobbing a car jacker?" Tracy asked.

"What exactly is 'jobbing'?"

"You know, a day job, like where you work."

"I don't have a job. My mechanic is not work."

"Well he's not exactly a vacation." Tracy shifted in her seat. "What's up with your mom? What got her so bent out of shape?"

"There's been a little trouble in paradise. I think the astronaut got dumped on the dark side of the moon."

"Really? What happened?"

"Dan got loosey-goosey in Vegas. Mom caught him making eyes at some other church ladies. He lost a lot of Brownie points."

"So she's taking it out on you."

"I guess."

"Did she find out about the party yet?"

"She's definitely suspicious. The cleanup committee missed a few empty beer bottles in the backyard."

"Blame it on those kids down the road."

"I already did."

"What did you tell her about the mechanic?"

"He's not a mechanic." I took a hit off the cigarette. "He's a race car driver."

"And you're just the all-American girl he probably thought he'd never have. A girl from the other side of the tracks bursting with repressed fantasies."

"I am not repressed!"

"Are so!"

"Well compared to you maybe."

I stared out the window, watching the sun fall behind the cornfields. Long shafts of blood-orange light swept through the hardy green stalks. I wasn't sure what to expect at the speedway, and at the same time I knew better than to have any expectations. Who knows what was going through Bobby's mind. He might have another girlfriend. He might have two or three.

SPEEDWAY

THE dirt lot was jammed with tailgate parties. People stood around smoky grills scorching hot dogs, burning hamburgers, washing it down with cold beer. Tracy found a parking spot out back near the edge of the woods. She was wearing white shorts, matching clogs, and a tight, pink baby doll top that curled over her pierced belly button like wrapping for expensive candy. Sporting a wicked tan, she had major accessories: a yellow plastic comb poking from her back pocket, a cloth ankle bracelet, and sparkle-silver fingernail polish. I looked kind of lame in comparison, wearing my faded blue summer dress and dirty pink Converse All Stars.

The speedway wasn't as fancy as I'd imagined. The track wasn't even paved. The lady at the gate looked like she'd been living in the ticket box for the last twenty years. One of her eyes was dead, so it seemed like she was looking both ways at the same time. She handed us two paper tickets, which were torn in half by the guy in the yellow windbreaker as we passed through the gate. Tracy and I walked under the bleachers to the pit area, where the cars were parked, but the security guard wouldn't let us into the back lot.

"No pit lizards until after the show." He smiled like someone you could never trust in a million years.

"Look!" Tracy pointed. "There he is. Coming out of the brown trailer."

Bobby was wearing a white leather bodysuit with various ad patches sewn onto his chest, a swooping cursive *Bobby* was stitched in red over his heart. He put on a red glitter helmet and climbed into his car, feet first, through the window. One of Bobby's friends from the garage closed the front hood and latched it with a thick chain and lock. The car ignited and roared to life. Bobby rolled out onto the track.

"C'mon." I took Tracy's hand, and we walked back toward the stands. "I'll buy you a beer."

We went back under the grandstand to the burger shack, a small open-faced trailer that sold cotton candy, peanuts, but mostly Miller beer. I ordered two, got carded, flashed the guy my fake ID. No problem. The sweaty paper cups were stuffed into a cardboard tray. I gave the old-timer his five bucks.

"It's so loud." Tracy held her hands over her ears.

The crowd was mostly guys in muscle tees and baseball hats, some farm boys, lots of spill from the petroleum plants, guys with beer guts and pink sweaty faces who like to drink until they pass out. We climbed up into the grandstand to find seats, and settled for an out-of-the-way place near the top. The rickety bleachers seemed to wobble every time the crowd got excited. Some of the benches were still sticky from the night before; scraps of snack-food—peanut shells and potato chip bits—were scattered all around. I pulled Tracy's comb from her pocket and gave my hair a fine-tuning.

Floodlights on huge wooden poles burned overhead. A fire truck was parked at one end of the track, and beside it was an ambulance with the back door propped open. The restraining walls were a series of billboards: Winston, Miller, Pepsi, Skoal, a local Jiffy Lube, an excavation company, and a gas station. The paint was peeling from all the signs, most of them severely outdated with logos from the past.

"So are you going to move in with the astronaut or is his family moving in with you?" Tracy asked.

"I told you, things didn't go so well in Vegas. It seems like the knight in shining armor lost some of his gleam. And even if they do patch it all up, Mom can't sell the house as fast as she shackled the astronaut." I cupped my chin in my hands, rested my elbows on my knees. "I'll be long gone by the time my mom's picking out new wallpaper patterns. I just hope she didn't blow it."

"I thought you hated the guy."

"Yeah, but it's better when she has a louse than no louse at all."

"How's your brother taking all this?"

"My brother's satellite needs new batteries."

"Your brother could be a god, that's his problem."

"If Jesus came back do you think he'd reincarnate as a rock star or a homeless person?"

"I think if he came back, he'd definitely keep a low profile. You heard what they did to him last time." Tracy looked into her beer cup.

"Let's get back to your brother. He's due for a relationship, right? I mean, now that your mom might marry Dan, he's a free man, right?" Tracy billowed a huge sigh, as if all the air had been let out of her balloon.

"That beach is closed. I don't know why you insist."

Tracy stared into the speedway lights and the patch of faint stars beyond them. "Maybe I'll go to college next fall and have an affair with my English teacher," she said, sounding more desperate than ever.

"What if he has hair on his back?"

"Nobody in my fantasies has hair on his back! Why do you always have to ruin everything, now I'll have to think up a new one."

"Like that'll be real hard."

Cars entered the dirt track one after the other. Revving down the straightaways, swerving around the corners, they didn't have the low rumble you'd expect, it was more of a high-pitched whine like giant lawn mowers circling the house. I set my beer on the bench in front of us and kept my hands cupped over my ears. A few cars were still in the pit area, getting last-minute adjustments from their crews. They all looked homemade, and the big fat tires reminded me of my brother's old Matchbox cars, each of them painted with colors as bright as a fishbowl: play school yellow and swimming pool blue, day-glo orange and cherry soda red.

Tracy pointed out a patch of manhood nearby, a couple guys in flannel shirts wearing blue jeans two sizes too big. They both wore their baseball caps backward, one with a feed-store brand and the other sporting John Deere's green and yellow.

"I think I'm developing a thing for gangsta farm boys,"

Tracy said. "I'll bet they drive pickup trucks and listen to Eazy-E."

I could tell Tracy was getting bored, so I offered to buy another round of beers. We bought a souvenir program, checked out all the blurry photographs of the other drivers. Nobody even came close to matching my mechanic, but Tracy found a few she might let drive her home. We sat on a picnic bench under the stands trying to avoid the noise, but it was everywhere. The ground was littered with red-and-white-striped popcorn boxes and sheer white hot dog wrappers. Tracy picked through the grass, looking for coins dropped from the pockets of people in the stands, but all she found was a lime green butane lighter.

We went and stood by the fence for the beginning of the race. The cars circled by in a single-file line behind an old green Chevy El Camino pace car with mag wheels. I recognized Bobby's car in the middle of the crowd. When they reached the far side of the track the green flag was waved, and they were off. One car after another zoomed by us. It was really loud and smoky. The lead car quickly lapped the last car, then it all got very confusing. It was hard to tell who was in front and who was in back, as well as how many laps had already been completed. I kept checking out Bobby, urging him on, keeping my fingers crossed that he didn't get hurt. An announcer barked the play-by-play through the ancient squawking P.A., but I couldn't understand a word of it.

Everything seemed orderly until the red car tried to pass the orange one and suddenly lost control and crashed into the yellow car near the last turn. The yellow car spun around in a circle and then hit the high wall and splattered into pieces. The crowd jumped to its feet and the bleachers shook wildly. It felt like the whole thing was going to come tumbling down. The red car rolled into the muddy infield and died, its engine spraying a geyser of steam. Bobby slipped through the wreckage unscathed and was near the front of the pack. The driver of the yellow car climbed out of his car and ran into the infield. A yellow flag came out, and all the remaining cars settled back into a single-file line, gliding around the track at a slower speed. A tow truck arrived and began to push the debris out of the way.

"This is gonna take a while," I said. "Let's go pee."

We went and stood in line for the Porta Pottis. The ground was muddy and it smelled so bad I had to hold my nose. I opened the door with my pinkie to avoid germs, tried squatting without touching anything. Murky light leaked through the floor vents, every surface seemed to shine with scum.

Tracy went after me. "I hate when there's no toilet paper," she said, coming out of the plastic booth, combing her shiny blond hair for about the zillionth time.

We went back toward the grandstand, standing for a while near the fence up front. The cars seemed dangerous up close, and the wheels threw up clods of dirt that sometimes shot through the fence. The green flag was waved and the cars went even faster. The blue car snuck up behind Bobby and squeezed him into the lower part of the track, then passed him on the outside. Around they went, side by side, bumper to bumper. On the next turn, Bobby tried to pass the blue car on the outside, but was sideswiped into the wall. A huge stream of orange sparks splashed over the restraining wall. Bobby held the car steady, but let up a bit around the turn. The blue car got caught in traffic and Bobby was immediately back on his case. Bobby faked like he was going to pass on the outside, but then slid down low on the inside of the dirt track and cut off the blue car. A massive cloud of powdery dust was forming overhead. I could taste little sandy bits in my mouth. Bobby was in second place, I think. I looked over at Tracy, she was getting into it.

"Did you see that move?" she asked.

The cars roared up the straightaways, then slid through the corners of the circular track. They seemed to be going faster as the race evolved. Bobby was putting serious pressure on the lead car, staying right on him, when all of a sudden, the gold car clipped the rear tire of the green one and scraped up against the near wall, giving everyone in the front rows a good scare.

"It would be just my luck to be killed by a flying tire or something," Tracy said. "I suggest we move back up into the bleachers." When I reminded her of the curse she walked all the way to the top.

"So what are we gonna do after the race?" Tracy was getting anxious.

"I'm sure there'll be some sort of party," I speculated.

"But what if he loses?"

The crowd jumped to its feet and burst into cheers when the announcer said there was only one more lap to go. The man in the tower swung a large white flag over the track, signaling the drivers. Bobby was right on top of the lead car, making moves like he wanted to pass. At the first turn, it seemed they were trying to push each other off the track. Around the back side Bobby went high and then tried to sweep down behind the lead car, but was cut off on the turn. The announcer's voice rose into a frantic scream as the two cars banked into the final stretch. The crowd was hollering at the drivers. Nose to nose, the cars grew louder and louder as they approached the finish line. People in the crowd were screaming. I couldn't tell who was going to win, but the barker yelled it out, "Number forty-seven, Tony Kaiser!" The crowd jumped up and down as the cars roared under the checkered flag. My beer went sailing down into the grass below.

"That was so close!" Tracy screamed. Bobby's car slowed down on the far side, and I could see him swearing all the way from here. We watched him roll past the grandstand, turn off the track, and park in the pit area beside the brown trailer.

"C'mon." I pulled Tracy by the arm. We wormed our way through the crowd toward the restraining wall's chicken-wire fencing. Tracy wanted to jump down onto the roadway, but I held her hand. We watched Bobby climb out of his car. He threw his red helmet on the ground and kicked the dirt.

"Looks like he's in a fun mood," Tracy said.

People began to file into the parking lot. The crowd was evaporating, the stands almost empty. We walked toward the pit. I saw Bobby's friends loading the car onto the trailer. Bobby stood beside the truck. He looked wired, like somebody who just got off a roller coaster.

"Hey, Bobby!" Tracy called out.

Bobby looked over. I waved my arm. He didn't seem to recognize us at first, but then smiled and walked over to the gate, pressed his fingers through the chain-link fence. I could tell he was sad.

"I didn't know you were here," he said.

"Well, thanks for inviting me," I protested.

"It was a last-minute thing." He sounded defeated, almost embarrassed. "Did you see me get my ass kicked again?"

"Looked like fun. Can I ride in the backseat next time?"

"Excuse me." Tracy tapped me on the shoulder.

"Bobby, this is my best friend Tracy." I introduced her.

"Hi," he said, giving her the once-over. Tracy tossed back her hair, letting him get the most of his inspection.

Bobby was preoccupied with losing and kept looking over at the winner and his crew standing around their car. "That fucker pushed me into the wall because he knew I was about to take him." He kicked his foot against the fence.

"Cheaters never feel good about winning," I said.

Bobby looked over at me. "How'd you guys find out about this?" he asked, suspicious and paranoid as ever.

"It was in the paper," I said.

I wondered if Bobby knew the cops were looking for him. Somebody must have tipped him off by now, somebody at the gas station. I wanted to bring it up, but there were a lot of people standing around.

"We're gonna have a few beers back at the garage," he said. "You want to come by?"

"She's driving," I said.

"How do we get there?" Tracy asked.

"Chrissie knows the way, right?" he looked at me.

"That charming spot across from the prison?" I asked.

He pressed his fingers through the fence and kissed me. "I'll see you there." He turned to pack the rest of his gear. I watched him walk away. A shiver started up the back of my arms and surged from one end of my nervous system to the other. Tracy grabbed my hand and led me out to the parking lot.

"You dare leave him alone in that silicone jungle?" Tracy asked.

"Men are like a bungee cord, they stretch as far as they can, but always bounce back safely."

"Yeah, but every once in a while you hear about one breaking."

"And then he's dead."

"What's the logic in that?"

"There is no logic in love."

We got in the car and Tracy started the engine, revving it good, then swerved into the exit line and snaked her way out of the speedway lot. The highway was refreshing after that dusty stadium and those stinky hot dogs. The cool night air gushed in the window, crept over my skin, turned it to shivery goose bumps.

"It's too bad he didn't win," Tracy said.

"Do you think he likes me?"

"It's a little soon for him to lay all his cards on the table."

"I laid all mine on the table."

"Guys always freak out when they get involved with someone. He probably just feels guilty or unworthy or both."

"Tracy, don't compare my boyfriends with yours, Rolex and Timex, get the picture?"

"You shouldn't have let him have all the candy the first time in the store. A guy like that gets more sweetie-pie than the whole football team put together, more lipstick on his dipstick than—"

"Thank you, that's enough."

THE GARAGE

THE two-lane blacktop road was broken on the edges like a worn leather belt, bushes on both sides were chewing away the shoulder, the faded yellow stripes looked like they'd been painted a hundred years ago. We passed the Legion Hall parking lot, which was packed. A small blinking sign near the road advertised THE ROADKILL PLAYBOYS.

At the stoplight a blue station wagon pulled up beside us. Henry Rollins music was thumping against the window. Inside the car were four boys pogoing on their seats.

"What do you think?" Tracy nodded toward them.

"They look like the stupid kind of wastoids who get gobbled up in the first ten minutes of a horror movie," I said.

"Is that a yes or a no?"

"That's a no, thank you very much."

"You are getting to be such a snob."

Tracy's future ex-husbands zoomed ahead when the light

turned green. Tracy putted along behind them. We passed the refinery fire, which was still lighting up the sky, but only drawing half the crowd. Even disaster gets boring after a while. Tracy gunned the VW over the rickety bridge and whipped a hard right down Archer Avenue. We drove past the refinery's glowing night shift, the Moose Lodge, Southwest Auto Salvage, Elks Lodge, Midway Tire, and the Hubcap Palace.

"Slow down. It's right around here somewhere." I kept my eyes peeled for the cigar tree, squinting at every intersection for familiar landmarks.

"There it is!" I pointed at the next corner. "Turn right."

Tracy downshifted and swerved toward the canal.

"It's the second driveway on the right."

Tracy stopped just shy of the mailbox. The garage door was open. A large confederate flag hung on the back wall. Murky blue light shone on three guys holding plastic beer cups, one pumping a keg, all of them squinting toward the glare of our unfamiliar headlights.

"Let's not stay too long," I said, trying to reel her in before she drank any more beer. Tracy raised an eyebrow at me, a sure sign of trouble. She turned off the car, pushed the door open, and grabbed her bag. I got out slowly and followed her into the garage.

"How's it goin'?" Tracy asked, waving her hand in the air like a tourist who didn't understand the language.

"A lot better since you all showed up. Who wants a beer?" The fat guy was cordial, almost grateful for our appearance. He handed each of us a foaming paper cup. Tracy sipped hers. I let mine spill over the top.

"We must be early," I said. "Where's Bobby?"

"On his way," the short one said. "Who are you?"

"Just a friend. I'm Chrissie and this is Tracy."

"I'm Kevin." He reached out his hand to shake mine. He had dry coarse hands, big though, for such a little guy. His eyes were black and seemed unable to focus on anything.

"This is Greg," he said, nodding toward the tall slouching skinny guy wearing a Jack Daniel's T-shirt. He didn't look very friendly and spit some tobacco juice into a stack of tires. "And that there's Danny." He pointed with his thumb toward the fat guy, who smiled ear to ear like a character in a children's book.

"Did ya see the race?" Danny asked.

We both nodded. "Sure was loud," Tracy said.

They all laughed like we were cute or something.

"Where's the bathroom?" I asked.

"First door on your right," Kevin said.

"So," Tracy said, clearing her throat, "how do I get a job racing cars?" They all laughed again.

I went through the doorway and down the hallway. Greasy black auto parts were stacked along the walls. A washer and dryer covered with dirty rags were tucked under some shelves holding a collection of pesticides, rusting cans of Black Flag and Raid.

The building smelled musty, like water damage had seeped through the roof and spread into the walls. The bathroom sink was almost black, the mirror a smudgefest, the toilet covered with yellow pee stains. Mold was eating up the shower curtain, spiderwebs hung above it. There was an old razor on the sink, a dirty yellow bar of soap, and opposite the toilet hung a MOPAR calendar with a picture of a topless blonde leaning over an old red car: Miss December.

I peed and flushed, pulled my underpants up in a hurry, wiped my hands on my dress, then walked back into the garage and rescued my beer.

"More Miller," Tracy said, kinda disappointed.

The beer was cold and the white suds felt comforting on my upper lip. My throat was still dusty from the racetrack and the beer coated my inside, hopefully killing all the germs I just inhaled in the john.

More cars began to fill up the driveway, mostly guys. They all approached the keg with comfortable familiarity. There was a tall slender woman with jet black hair and a dragon tattoo slithering up her arm who stood out from all the rest. She was wearing black vinyl boots with matching fingernails, purple lipstick, two-tone Asian eye shadow, and a perfume that sucked all the fresh air out of the garage. Her skin was pale, almost purplish, and she worked that Addams Family style, like Morticia from Bolingbrook. She looked like the queen of some suburban coven or the owner of an exotic flower shop, one that sold orchids and Venus's-flytraps.

"Where's Bobby?" Tracy whispered. I shrugged my shoulders, found an old tire to sit on. Tracy leaned against the wall. Danny came and sat on a tool chest beside us. He wore a black T-shirt under a purple polyester shirt and black Wranglers. A gold eagle belt buckle bigger than my fist saddled his swelling belly. His glasses were tinted blue, and his greasy blond hair hung halfway down his back. He was missing a finger on his left hand and I tried not to stare.

"How long have you known Bobby?" he asked.

"Just a couple of weeks," I said. "I met him at the gas station."

"That's how I met him." Danny laughed. I got the feeling he would have laughed at anything I said.

The dragon lady was staring at me, as if she wanted to burn my eyes out with her cigarette.

"What's her problem?" I asked.

"That's Asha Lorenza. I'm afraid she's got eyes for Bobby too." He glanced her way. "And I think she's been on the waiting list a little longer than you have. Bobby ran a hell of a race tonight. He was inspired. I believe Asha has sniffed out our boy's new blood." He looked at me like some jaded uncle, as if he'd seen this psychodrama played out several times before. I blushed red as cherry Kool-Aid. He tapped my beer cup with his, we bonded. Tracy tapped mine and killed the rest of hers.

"Want another one?" Tracy asked.

"Sure she does." Danny cheered.

Tracy walked over to the keg, made eyes at me, looked over at this cute guy with sandy blond hair wearing a faded blue Levi's jacket, then back at me. I shook my head no and she laughed.

"So how'd you hook up with Bobby?" I asked Danny.

"I work the parts counter in the yard." He took a hit off his beer. "Bobby brings in a lot of wrecks scraped off the highway. We got to know each other pretty good. He was always talking about racing. One night I got so drunk I guess I promised to build him a car." Danny laughed again.

"Wasn't there another driver before Bobby?" I asked.

"Bobby's the only one crazy enough to get in that car. He's been fearless. He might actually win one of these nights."

"Tonight was so close," I said. "I almost had a heart attack."

"Me too!" He laughed.

"Is he a good driver?"

"He ain't dead yet." Danny laughed again. "I'm usually just happy to see him come back alive. It may not be the fastest car, but it holds together."

"Where do you suppose he is?" I asked.

"Starting to wonder myself," he said.

I shifted on the tire, worried that he was arrested, that the cops were about to raid this pit stop any second now. I wondered what Danny knew and whether I should tell him what I did, but I wasn't sure where Bobby drew his borders and I didn't want to go anywhere without a passport.

"I'll be right back." I got up and walked around the keg to the other side of the garage, looking for Tracy, but didn't see her anywhere. I didn't see the guy with the Levi's jacket either. She doesn't waste any time.

Danny got off the tool chest and approached some of Asha's groupies. All of a sudden I was the wallflower at the kegger. There were a few guys staring at me, but most of them resembled wanted posters in the post office, so I went and hid in the bathroom. Beer makes me pee as fast as I drink it. I gave myself a fresh dose of lip gloss and whispered a mantra to the disciple of future boyfriends, but when I opened the door, I came face-to-face with Asha Lorenza. Flashing an *über* evil smile, her icy vampire breath purred at the soft veins of my throat. I retreated a step, leaned against the doorway, fumbled for a cigarette.

"You scared me," I said.

"I scare a lot of girls," she said. "So what's your name?"

"Chrissie," I said. "It's a pleasure to meet you."

We stared at each other through an awkward silence. She was sizing me up for a coffin, and I was looking for a weapon to put an end to the wicked witch of the Midwest. Where the fuck was Bobby?

"So how long have you and Bobby been friends?" she asked.

"A while."

"Did you find him or did he find you?"

"I pulled into the gas station. He came to my window. Do you know where he is?"

"He just called. Apparently the trailer had a flat tire. He said he'd meet us down at the Roadhouse."

"You mean that strip joint out on Frontage Road? Why would he want to go there?"

"I own the place." She smiled. "Do you need a lift?"

"I have a ride, thanks." I started to walk away.

"Should I tell Bobby you're on your way?" she asked.

I went down the hallway, through the garage and circled the empty keg. No Tracy. I walked to the end of the driveway. Tracy's car was gone. She had abandoned me, and now everyone was abandoning the party. There were a few stragglers hanging out in the corners, but nobody I wanted to get to know any better, so I made casual toward Asha's car.

"Is there still room for me?" I asked.

Asha rolled down her window. "Sorry, babe," she said, "this one's full, try the one behind us."

I walked over to the other car. Some gangly greaseball with

green teeth and scrawny shoulders rolled down the window. His buddies were staring at me like a car full of retarded serial rapists.

"Can you guys give me a lift?" I asked. The car door popped open, no questions asked. This was the luckiest day of their lives, and it's all Tracy's fault if I end up on the back of a milk carton. I looked back at the empty garage wondering whether I should reconsider, then bent down and climbed into the backseat. The car smelled like pot. The door slammed shut, the driver shifted into reverse and backed out of the driveway. The wagon train sped off to the strip club.

"You wanna get stoned?" the guy next to me asked. His eyes were red as Life Savers, swollen like a pair of catcher's mitts.

"No thank you." I passed it up front. The car sailed along with Marilyn Manson cranked. The guy on the other side was playing air guitar.

"So are you a dancer or something?" the stoner asked.

"Or something," I said.

"Wow." His eyes nearly popped out of his head. "I never met a something before." The whole car cracked up: stoner joke extraordinaire.

The driver turned up the stereo, started singing along, and so did the guy riding shotgun, and before long the backseat joined in at the chorus.

"You guys should start a Marilyn Manson tribute band," I said mockingly.

They just sang louder, the guy in front screaming at the chorus. Fucking idiot wanna-bes. I'm going to kill Tracy.

THE ROADHOUSE

THE caravan slowed down just before the Interstate bridge and turned left onto Frontage, a dark two-lane road that ran parallel to the highway then dipped back into the woods. Two white aphrodite statues guarded the driveway of the Roadhouse, a two-story barn with a satellite dish on the roof. A small red bulb glowed over the doorway. The sign above it read TOPLESS in gold neon script. There were a lot of motorcycles near the front door, a pair of sixteen-wheelers at the far end of the lot, a hot rod, and a couple beaters in between. I didn't see Bobby's car anywhere.

The stoners piled out of the car like their seats were on fire. I was feeling a little uneasy, wondering where Bobby was, where Tracy was, and where I was, for that matter. Asha's car pulled into the lot and parked beside us. I trailed the stoner boys inside, pausing in the doorway to scan the room. There was an empty seat at the near end of the bar and it seemed like every guy in the place watched me find it. I stood out like a Corvette in a used-car lot. Asha and her committee entered behind me. The bartender came over and asked for my ID. I flashed my fake one.

"Are you a cop?" he asked me point-blank.

"No." I shook my head.

"Arthur!" Asha screamed over the music. The bartender turned around. "She's with me!" Asha pointed at me. He threw the ID on the bar.

"Okay, Shirley Temple, what do you want?" he asked.

"Rum and Coke," I shouted out.

"I should have guessed." He filled a glass with ice, poured the rum, and then spritzed it with the spray gun. He plopped in a couple maraschino cherries and dropped the glass in front of me, then went off to take care of Asha's crowd. I turned and glanced around the bar.

Two women were onstage wearing bits and pieces of cheap lingerie, strutting to some *Saturday Night Fever* song. The room was full of rednecks nodding along to disco, one of them swinging around like some perverted farmer doing the jig for his pigs. His jeans were drooping as he danced around in front of the stage, flashing the crack of his rear. Finally he spun around one time too often and did a corkscrew into a table. When he crashed onto the floor the room erupted with laughter, even the girls onstage were laughing.

The door swung open, and I leaned toward it anticipating Bobby, but it was just another pack of ex-convicts, hot and horny after twenty years in the pen. The last one wore an eyepatch like a pirate. They crossed the room, paused at the far end of the bar to order a pitcher of Old Style, then proceeded to take over the pool table. Asha came toward me, stirring her drink with a red swizzle stick. She parked in the chair beside me and admired herself in the mirror behind the bar. Her perfume just about made me gag.

"So what do you think?" she asked.

"Fun place." I tried to smile.

"A girl like you could make a lot of money in a club like this." She popped open her black vinyl pocketbook, fished out a glass cigarette case, offered me one. I accepted.

"What are you saying?"

"Aren't you looking for a job?" She looked puzzled, flicked her lighter.

I dipped my cigarette into the fire.

She tucked the lighter back into her purse. The shifting contents revealed a tiny silver pistol tucked in the red jaws of her bag.

"I don't think I have a big enough ego." I glanced at the door, looking for a miracle.

Asha leaned against the bar, drawing a hit from her mile-long cigarette. She had a cool calculated delivery, as if everything was rehearsed or had been said a million times before. "It's easy money," she said, blowing smoke rings toward the rafters.

"Not easy enough," I said. "I don't like getting naked in front of myself, let alone the entire criminal population of Will County."

"What about your friend? She could be a headliner." Asha sipped her drink, letting it all soak in.

"I'll ask her next time I see her." I turned and watched the next girl drop her skirt to the floor, swinging her hips like some superwhore at senior prom. Prancing back and forth in black high heels, acting as coy as a child in an ice cream parlor, her metallic underwear refracted thin white beams of light that bounced around the smoky room.

"Where's Bobby?" I asked.

"He's probably somewhere he shouldn't be, or worse." She stared at my breasts, as if I were flat and self-conscious or something. She of course was flawless, if you have a fetish for forty-year-old vampire babes who smell like cats. Asha set her glass on the bar, dropped her cigarette onto the floor, and crushed it with her toe.

"Let me know when you're ready for your audition." She turned and disappeared through a red door in the back of the room. I crushed my cigarette in the ashtray, swirled in my seat, took inventory of the memorabilia ornamenting the back of the bar.

Tacked to the wall was an old poster from when the speedway first opened. The car in the center was nice and blurry to accentuate the thrill of speed. Over the mirror hung a string of miniature plastic tiki lights, the heads of Easter Island in red, green, and yellow. At the base of the mirror was a line of sticky bottles, all the usual suspects. There was a cash register in the center, surrounded by cyanamide strips, glowing green and orange like radioactive IVs. A couple of Polaroids of girls holding their shirts up were taped to its side. The bartender avoided me, working the opposite end of the room, chatting up the pirate and his gang.

I was starting to have some serious doubts about the mechanic showing up anytime soon. Stuck like bait in an alligator cage, my chair was starting to feel a little wobbly. I couldn't figure out whether Asha was his past or present girlfriend. She obviously had some history, even if there wasn't any future.

I watched the dancers in the mirror, wondered if they lived nearby, if they shopped at SaveMart with a handful of coupons and flipped through the rags while waiting their turn at the checkout line, whether they had a social life outside the club, a place to wind down after dressing up like sluts and whipping the town drunks into a rousing state of frenzied horniness.

The room was scattered with some of the biggest losers this side of I-55. I didn't dare look up, because the last time I did, that sweaty pirate-looking creature was focused on me like a cat about to snatch a bird. He gave me the creeps, and I suddenly felt the need to be rescued. It was time to gather up my marbles and get the hell out of here. The door swung open and I looked up, hoping it was Bobby, but it was the boys I had crushed with the car battery. I had a heart attack. My valentine was wearing a neck brace. I buried my face in my cocktail and watched them in the mirror as they entered the room. I started sweating big-time. I slid off the edge of my seat, leaned down, and pretended to tie my shoe. They stopped in front of the stage and stood stonefaced, staring at the naked girls onstage. Nobody seemed to notice me, so I decided to take a chance, grabbbed my bag, and ducked out into the parking lot.

I wasn't sure what to do. Neither Tracy's nor Bobby's car was in the lot, and the only person I knew inside was the vampire madam from hell. Mosquitoes swarmed around my forehead, buzzing in and out of my ears. The roar of sixteen-wheelers shifting gears echoed from the highway, the carnival lights of their trailers whipped through the trees. Music was thumping against the door when all of a sudden it burst open. I looked over my shoulder and saw Mr. Neckbrace limping toward me. I pressed my back against a car and slowly back-pedaled away from him.

"Well, well, well, look what we have here. I thought that was you. Remember me?" he asked, casually sinister, like someone who just crawled out of the swamps of Cape Fear. I shook my head, watched his hands.

"No. Why should I?"

"Don't play dumb with me sister." He kept taking baby steps toward me. "Your locker was just the beginning. Let's just hope there isn't an accident before graduation."

"What are you talking about?"

"The curse." He laughed. "We got big plans for you."

A white car swung into the lot, and its headlights swept the front of the building. I turned and ran toward the car and then straight past it until I was out of the parking lot.

"It won't be long now!" he called out.

I kept running. I didn't dare turn around. My heart was racing and I couldn't think clearly because I was cluttered with panic. Thick patches of weeds made both sides of the road impenetrable. The stop sign at the corner was punctured by a dozen bullet holes. Suddenly I was the girl in a horror movie. My eyes puckered with tears. I was really really scared.

I couldn't hear his feet, but I had a constant sinking feeling they were right behind me. Whenever I turned around, how-ever, there was only a halo of streetlight glaring down at the pavement. Nothing was moving along the road, and the silence only frightened me more. I hurried under the Interstate bridge and started up Lemont Road, keeping a steady pace. Whenever

headlights jumped over the horizon, I dipped into the shadow
of trees. I didn't want to give him a second chance.

Dark clouds had buried the stars. Tree branches above started
to rock back and forth, bending with the force of an invisible
wind. That's when I felt the first drop of rain slap the end of
my nose. At the next streetlight I started feeling drops all over
my arms and legs, and by the time I reached the one after that,
I was soaking head to toe.

Rain fell like the rivers of heaven had crested, on and on
with increasing intensity. Puddles quickly became channels of
gushing water alongside the road. Lightning sliced across the
sky, thunder crept closer, each time with slightly more intensity, until the storm seemed to be right on top of me. I started
worrying about getting electrocuted under the tall trees lining
the road, so I cut across the street and followed the edge of the
cornfield.

My mind stayed busy racing through the serial killer trading
cards, as if Neckbrace didn't get me, somebody else would. As
the streetlight up ahead grew brighter, my fears would dimin-
ish, but as soon as I passed it and walked deeper into darkness,
all that fear came racing back. And then a sheet of lightning
reached out of the sky and sucked all the electricity out of
Downers Grove. The streetlights failed and it got real dark, so
dark I couldn't even see myself. Standing completely still, waiting for my eyes to adjust, I felt like a ghost, like I wasn't even
alive. Everything seemed so unreal. Headlights and taillights
became the only beacons that shredded the night, and I followed them, cautiously.

By the time I made it home I was so exhausted I felt like I
might die anyway. The power was still out and the whole

neighborhood seemed haunted. It was so unbelievably black. Lightning occasionally took a picture, but the snapshots seemed vacant and dreamlike.

The door was open to our house. I went inside and felt my way toward the kitchen. I heard some voices giggling, turned, and saw a warm glow emanating from the basement. There were enough candles along the staircase to make Anne Rice drool. Water was lapping against the bottom stair. It looked like a cave.

"What's going on down there?" I started down the stairs and found David floating on a Styrofoam cooler, like some Hollywood surfer. His friend Dylan was sitting on a table with a large red bong glued to his face. My brother's beer can collection floated around them.

"Ahoy," my brother said, paddling with one hand while holding a can of beer in the other. "Grab a life preserver. The house is sinking."

"Where are the buckets?" I asked.

David looked around him. "Where is my boom box?"

Dylan held the bong toward me. "Want one?" he asked.

"No thanks," I said. "What happened?"

"We were playing cards when all of a sudden the electricity went out. The sump pump quit, and seconds later the water started coming up through the drain. We rounded up some candles and flashlights, and then tried to bail for a while, but it was pointless, so we just saved what we could. Where the hell have you been?" he asked.

"Out with Tracy."

"Mom had a shit fit when you pulled that disappearing act. She thinks you ran off with Speed Racer." He paddled toward me. "She said if you ever did show up you'd be grounded for life."

"I don't have a life, remember?"

"Hey, don't get harsh on me, I'm just the messenger."

"Where is she now?"

"Dan came by, I guess he's gonna lend her a car."

Dylan nodded his head, as though that's how he remembered it too.

"Did they patch things up?" I asked.

"I didn't know it was broken," he said.

I felt light-headed, like a piece of butter melting into warm toast. My stomach felt queasy, and then my head frosted over like the inside of a fluorescent bulb. Everything swirled into a soft blur. I swayed from one side to the other, then the whole world faded to black.

THE CONSPIRACY
THEORY

I told you, that party looked as permanent as a trailer park," Tracy said. "How did I know everyone was going to split? I took the white angel on a cigarette run, and when I came back the only people left were Bobby and his friend."

"What friend?" I asked.

"It was a guy," she said, as if reading my mind. "They had a flat tire. I would've killed myself if anything had happened to you." She squeezed my hand.

"Yeah, right." I pulled my hand away.

Fainting is so dramatic, but actually, I don't remember much of it. My brother said he could relate because he can't remember a lot of things too. He must have been a little freaked to see me more petrified than him. Mom was beside herself with anger and relief, in other words, she wanted to kill me but was glad I wasn't dead.

"I thought you were gonna be the senior curse," Tracy said.

"Well, I almost was. Asha lured me over to her nightclub and guess who showed up—the boys who kissed the car battery. Chuckie had a neckbrace. He followed me out into the parking lot and said the locker fire was just the beginning, that I was an accident waiting to happen."

"He's just trying to frighten you."

"Well, it worked. I had to walk all the way home in the biggest rainstorm of the century. I thought the world was ending. I was so scared. I cried and prayed all the way home."

"You didn't cry or pray," she said.

"How would you know? You were busy getting felt up by Stranger Danger."

"First of all, we only went to get cigarettes. Second of all, if I go away I always come back. You're the one who ditched me. Nobody said the party was going to be transient."

"You're the one who got me into this mess," I said.

"Me?"

"It was your idea to go to that party. It was your idea to throw the car battery!"

"Listen. Just chill, all right. If they try anything I will personally swat their agenda back in their face, just like last time, *comprende*?" Tracy tried to be reassuring, but her war speech was loosing its intensity. She seemed to think that this was all my fault and she was putting in overtime as it is.

Mom spent the night at Cape Canaveral, so Tracy took the honor of driving me to school and nearly got us both killed twice, making fast left turns in front of traffic. She had a remarkable way of bringing me right back into the danger zone.

I turned up the Bowie tape, sat back, and braced myself for an imminent collision.

We got stopped at the railroad tracks and watched a freight train rumble through town. The cars tilted back and forth with a slow and easy sway.

"Someday I'm gonna jump one of those suckers," Tracy said, "and ride it until the sun comes up."

"And then what?"

"I'll jump off."

"What are you gonna do in Nebraska?"

"Every time I have a fantasy you have to castrate it, why is that?"

"Well I was just pointing out that if you rode a train from here until sunrise you probably wouldn't be any farther than Nebraska."

"Since when are you the reality doctor?"

Tracy seemed to be in a foul mood, so I didn't push any more buttons. When we pulled into the school parking lot I was struck with panic. Finals were breathing down my neck and the books stacked beside my bed looked like the Sears Tower. Tracy was more concerned with fanzine no. 4 and started reviewing the finished pages of the next issue.

"I know it's a bit incestuous, but I still think we should put you on the cover," she said. "The locker fire is definitely top story."

"We should hold publication until the curse happens."

"You're right, we should wait for the curse. But what if it doesn't happen?"

"Then it's still the top story. I don't want to be on the cover, okay?"

"You know everyone is going to say it's a cover-up."

My locker was still a heap of rubble so I had to carry what was left of my books around all day in a big canvas bag. Tracy went to her fashion final and I went off to deal with French verbs. I took French as some sort of romantic concept. Listening to all those Françoise Hardy songs, I wanted to run off to Paris and become a poet or a terrorist, but when that plane crash happened with all those schoolkids inside, the whole dream became sort of haunted.

After class I met Tracy in the locker room.

"How did you do on your test?" I asked.

"I wrote an essay on the cross-pollination of Versace and Versailles called 'The Mirror and the Flashbulb.' It's a rambling swatch of ideas on gaudy behavior, but hopefully there are enough inspired moments of clarity to swing a passing grade."

We went to gym class and struggled through endless sit-ups and push-ups. I was actually pretty good with jumping jacks. Tracy and I both had a crush on Miss Thompson. I totally admired her style. A lipstick lesbian according to Tracy. Fishnet feminist according to me.

"Only you two could get a C in gym class," Miss Thompson said.

POWER LINES

ALL alone, scribbling long purple paragraphs into my journal—*Chrissie Bright, Chrissie Dark*—I felt inspired but was still very hesitant to commit anything to paper. I tried writing in code but ended up tearing out all those pages. I decided to leave a couple blank pages, and fill in the details once the scenery became more acceptable. So part of my journal will be filled with white lies, but better a crown of thorns than an execution, that's what I say.

There's always been plenty of material to draw from, but lately it's been one gush after another. First of all, my mechanic was still missing in action. What started as a desire to jump-start my life has since straddled me into a nonexistent relationship that continues to haunt me, especially at night. I've never been this stupid over a guy—ever. Plus, it's only a few days before graduation, and the curse has not been fulfilled. Maybe it won't happen this year? Maybe the gods are finally satisfied?

Maybe all the other accidents were just a coincidence? It totally creeped me out when Tracy said I should be on the cover of fanzine no. 4. It was such a bad omen.

Lying on my back, watching the alien-green numbers of my digital clock jump forward, I had so much adrenaline pumping through my system that it was impossible to sleep. Tossing and turning into the early morning hours, I finally crawled from my bed and lumbered downstairs, pushed the sliding door open, and headed for the willow tree.

The yard felt spookier on a moonless night—more shadows, more movement in the corner of my eye. I accidentally stepped on a rotten pear and its soft belly squished between my toes. The sweet wet scent reminded me of when Mom used to can fruit. That was back when Dad was still mowing the lawn. He loved the yard and spent most every Saturday afternoon snipping branches, raking leaves, and picking weeds. He even built a compost pile and started a garden. The rabbits ate it all, but Dad didn't really care, "as long as someone appreciated it," he said. That was the way my parents talked to each other, broadcasting their bitterness far above our heads, constantly struggling for our psychological favor while battling their own. The yard was the first thing to deteriorate, then slowly but surely the house became a reflection of the yard. Mom and Dad were overextended, and in the end they both lost interest in preserving their Camelot. It was a castle of frustration for both of them.

There were a few moments of sunshine and some were even preserved on Super 8 film. Dad thought he was the Godard of DuPage County, so all the footage is a little jumpy, like someone was playing hot potato with the camera. "Avant-garde," he called his masterpieces. "You were drunk," my mother would reply. I never thought of Dad as a drinker, but I guess a lot happened after we went to bed at night. How they got so bitter probably started long before I turned thirteen, but that's about when I began picking up their transmissions, and a couple of years later that's how it ended: one person trying to explain their bad behavior and the other one crucifying them for it. Neither one of them was happy with the life they had, so Dad split and went looking for a new one. Nothing ever exploded, it just sort of dissolved. I guess you could say the feelings were mutual. Mom acted as if she didn't care, but even now you can sense a part of her is missing.

All of the bickering left me with a huge sense of guilt, like it was my fault or something. Maybe if I had been more grateful at Christmas, or did the dishes a little more often, or got better grades, their life would not have disintegrated. Maybe it was up to me to shore up all the foundations and seal the cracks with love. "The cracks were so big you could've fallen right into them," Mom said. "You'll never know."

Why would I never know? Wouldn't I grow up to be just like her and experience all the same pain again if she didn't flash me a few cue cards? Seems to me that men are as wild and impossible as life itself.

I ducked under the lilac bushes and entered the umbrella of the willow tree's drooping branches, then started climbing up the fat trunk. Before I reached the top I saw a strange white light underneath the power lines that drooped over the corn-field. It looked like a fuzzy white angel was glowing in the sprouting field. I just about shit in my pants. Whatever it was, it wasn't moving. I wondered if it fell out of the sky and was hiding. I hurried down the tree.

Maybe angels were scavengers and spend all night stealing corn for banquets in heaven? Everything had a reason, and this seemed entirely reasonable at the moment. I thought about running back to the house and getting a camera, but my curiosity and excitement were too overwhelming. I crossed the street and slowly made my way along the edge of the field, then cut through a wide row of cornstalks, toward the bright white light.

There, in the middle of the field, was my grandmother, standing on a rock, holding a glowing white fluorescent tube above her head. She had a smile on her face as big as Montana, as though she were expecting both me and a large crowd to show up any minute.

"Chrissie, come here, you gotta try it!" Grandma waved me over with her free hand and I hesitantly made my way toward her.

"Where's it plugged in?" I asked.

"It's not," she said.

"How'd you do that?"

She pointed at the power lines up above.

"I thought you were an angel," I said, somewhat disappointed, somewhat relieved, shielding my eyes from the weird glow.

"What makes you think I'm not?" She laughed to herself. "Here." She held the bulb in my direction. "It won't hurt you."

Fat white moths were dancing around the slender white tube and big black bats were right behind them. I looked up at the transmission towers on either end of the field and the buzzing snake of wire hanging overhead. "I don't think so."

Grandma looked insulted.

"Where'd you learn that trick?" I asked.

She shrugged her shoulders. "Made it up, I guess."

"And what if your trick had killed you?"

"Then I'd be dead, but I'm not, am I?" She looked up at her white sword and smiled at its strange beauty. Grandma was getting weirder by the hour.

"Why are you wandering around in your pajamas again? And what's going on over at that house? I saw police cars on the cul-de-sac. There were so many lights flashing through the yard it looked like a UFO had landed."

"David had a party and the police came by."

"Was somebody murdered?"

"One of the neighbors probably complained that David's band was too loud."

"Wasn't me." She turned the tube sideways, and the large white fan of light evaporated into solid black. My eyes went fuzzy while adjusting to the sudden darkness. Grandma clasped her arm around mine and led me back through the field.

"So tell me about Mr. Troublemaker. I hear he's a race car driver."

"You'd like him, Grandma. I saw him race at Santa Fe Speedway."

"Did he win?

"No, but it was close."

"Are you falling in love?"

"I'm trying, but it's not easy. Every time I take a step closer, he takes two steps farther back."

"So take twice as many steps." Grandma swatted some flying insect away from her forehead.

"I wish it was that easy."

"Sounds to me like he's riding a roller coaster and you're waiting in line to buy a ticket. There's a big gap between those two comets. Maybe you should concentrate on your own tornado instead of trying to fight the wind in his," she said.

"Do you think he's like my father?"

Grandma tilted toward her house, leaning as far away from the question as possible. She punched her lips out and resituated her dentures, leading me across the road and up the gravel driveway.

"Do you know where he lives?" I asked.

She looked up at the sky. "I got a postcard from him once."

"Can I see it?"

She hesitated for a minute, then shook her head. "It's in one of those bottomless drawers."

"Where was it from?"

"Chicago," Grandma said. "You ever been there?"

"A couple of times—for concerts and stuff."

"You should check out the laser show at the planetarium," she said.

"You went to see the laser show?"

"Pink Floyd is the best." Grandma smiled. "You like Pink?" she asked.

"I like Pink."

She gave her denture plate another tumble. "I'll go find that card for you, but don't you ever tell your mother where it came from, promise?"

"Promise."

THE WINDY CITY

WITH a little pleading I convinced Tracy into taking a road trip. I was anxious to see my dad, and Tracy was looking for an excuse to blow off homework.

"I love going to Chicago," she said. "It makes me feel so dangerous."

We slipped onto the highway and evaporated into the hundreds of other identical cars. Tracy whipped through traffic on the Eisenhower Expressway, changing lanes with the furious pace of a windshield wiper.

My life was beginning to feel like an emotional Tilt-A-Whirl, up and down, around and around. Somehow I imagined that if I could bring Dad back into the picture everything else would fall into order.

"I don't think spying is cool." Tracy interrupted my space-out. "You should call your dad, tell him you're in the neighborhood, ask him to meet for coffee. It's the least you can do."

"Oh yeah right." I put my right hand up to my ear, as if I were talking on the phone. "Hey, Dad, it's me, Chrissie. Your daughter, remember? Well I just happened to be around the corner, yeah, and I just happened to have found your phone number in my pocket." I hung up the phone. "It's too obvious. Besides, I only want to see him. I don't want him to see me."

Tracy drove under the post office building and all of a sudden the expressway ended and we were on a four-lane street surrounded by skyscrapers. The sidewalks were barren except for the occasional misfit pushing a shopping cart. An electric train rumbled overhead. A great cloud of noise hung over the intersection.

Tracy turned left and accelerated up Lake Shore Drive. I cracked my window a bit to get a whiff of lake air. It smelled like vacations. Tracy exited at North Avenue, then headed north toward Wicker Park, to an after-hours club she had discovered surfing the Net one day at school. We parked on a dark treeless side street and walked back around the block.

"You know I should be home studying," Tracy said.

"Yeah right."

It was a nondescript brick building, but the windows sparkled with colorful flashing lights and we could hear music thumping inside. A pair of rocker sluts fell out of the doorway as we walked up, practically swallowing each other's pierced tongues.

"Is this a lesbian bar?" I whispered to Tracy.

"I hope not." She shrugged.

The bouncer checked our ID's, stamped our wrists, then opened the silver door. The room was lit with black light. The walls were painted in psychedelic patterns. Go-go dancers were perched on the bar, cranking to some industrial techno. I couldn't make out if they were boys or girls. The bar was lined with twenty-something beauties. Boys mostly, in leather and suede, some wearing makeup, some with white trash merit badges needled into their arms, everyone holding a long-neck bottle of beer. Junkies filled up all the negative spaces. There was a band playing some high-octane megatrash upstairs. Tracy grabbed my hand and led me through the crowd to a small courtyard out back. The El train screamed overhead, and it was deafening. We sat on some musty brown couch. I propped my knees up to my chin. Tracy peered around for familiar faces, hunting for a rock star, a movie star, or anything relatively similar.

"What'll we do now?" I asked.

"You should call your dad."

"You call him if you're so curious."

"This was your idea—remember?" Tracy stared around the courtyard like it was dinnertime. She might have even propositioned one of the gorgeous barflys if she had a little more time. The purple hickeys from her last conquest haven't even healed before she's on to the next one.

"Let's go upstairs," Tracy said. "I feel like trawling."

We climbed the rickety stairs to a one-hundred-degree room packed wall to wall with brand-new Sids and Nancys, a milk white late-night crowd of pierced and branded thrift store bandits. The girl beside me wore a Louise Brooks wig, a white rubber dress, and silver accessories: necklace, polish, and shoes. Stale beer and sweat seemed to be the predominant odors, but I could smell incense burning somewhere in the distance.

The lead guitarist played the opening lick of the next song;

a sweet psychedelic introduction that teased the audience. Everyone leaned forward slightly, anticipating a wall of noise. A blue spotlight focused on the tall skinny guitarist. He was shirtless. Long blond hair hung in front of his face. His instrument was cocked perfectly on his hip. The drummer and bass player kicked into some slamming hardcore, and the room exploded in moshing madness. The singer burst onstage with his head on fire and took out all three microphone stands, finally crashing into the side speaker cabinets. A roadie doused him with a fire extinguisher. White powder floated up into the lighting gear hanging above. He was wearing a bulletproof vest and a large white wig that was now stinking up the room bigtime. The singer ripped off his wig and latched on a steel army helmet, then lunged headfirst into the crowd. The things boys will do for attention.

Tracy looked at me with a big smiley face. She was totally into it. The singer was shoved back onto the stage and he spun around and around, shaking like he was having an epileptic seizure. The guitarist returned to the opening lick. The singer grabbed a microphone and launched into the first verse:

> So many possibilities
> I haven't got a clue,
> I don't believe in anything
> It's sad, I know, but true.
> My life is all so meaningless
> Our futures all are doomed
> I might as well go kill myself
> There's nothing else to do!

He dove headfirst back into the mosh pit. The crowd held him aloft like some fragile deity, then propelled him back onstage. His arms were extended in a crucifixion pose, his eyes rolled over, exposing whites, like he was possessed or about to puke. The singer pointed into the audience, picked up a microphone, and started repeating the chorus.

All my friends are nobodies
So who the fuck are you?
I might as well go kill myself
There's nothing else to do!

Tracy yelled into my ear, "Fucking intense or what?"

I was thinking about my dad, my mechanic, and my mom, not to mention graduation, and the curse. I expected Neckbrace and his lunatics to show up here at any minute. It was impossible to have fun. Everyone around me looked so bent on irresponsibility. Glancing around the room, it was hard for me to get enthusiastic. Some guy fell out of the crowd and painted Tracy's arm with sweat.

"Gross!" She wiped her arm on her pants leg.

I lured her over to the side bar and bought a couple beers, handed one to Tracy. The microbrew was thick as plasma, the air choked with secondhand smoke. I was anxious to spin by my dad's house.

"At least I want to see the building," I said, "to get a sense of it."

Tracy got bored after a few more songs and finally agreed to go, but only after I promised we could check out another club on the West Side afterward. We slammed the rest of our beers and retired back to the sidewalk.

"I can't wait until we move down here," Tracy said. "We are gonna be so famous."

"For what?"

"For us."

We jumped back into the Volkswagen and headed downtown. Two-story brick buildings were stacked one after another, dark alleyways ran between them. Large drooping elm trees deflected the streetlights. It was a spooky place, at this hour anyway.

"What's the number again?" Tracy downshifted on Belmont, peering over the dashboard.

"Six-five-four," I said.

"There it is." She pointed to a brown brick building.

It wasn't what I expected. I don't know what I expected, but I know I envisioned something bigger and livelier. The building seemed dark and unimpressive, more ominous than glamorous. The good news was that it looked like there might be some lights on in the first-floor window. Tracy pulled over at the corner.

"I should go with you," she said.

"No. Wait here. I'll be right back." I popped the door open and hurried up the block. There were a lot of dark green bushes and I felt discreet, but I wasn't quite sure what I was hiding from. I stopped at the doorway, but there weren't any names on the mailboxes. The hallway was littered with supermarket flyers and take-out menus for Chinese food. The glass door was locked. I rang the first bell, then rang another one, wondering whether I should leave before it was too late. Who was going to benefit from this? How would I explain myself? What if he's with another woman? What if he's wasted? When I turned away from the door the porch light went on. I froze. I heard the door swing open, so I spun around and was face-to-face with someone older than my grandma.

"Can I help you?" she asked. The woman peered, semi-trembling, from behind a chained door. I glanced down at her ancient slippers.

"I'm looking for a guy, sorta tall, his name is Terry Swanson."

"He doesn't live here." She started to close the door.

"Did he move?"

She backed farther out of sight.

"I'm looking for my father," I blurted out.

The old woman peered through the crack in the door. "What makes you think he's here?"

"I was told he lived here."

"My husband died seven years ago. You say he's your father?"

"No, I'm sorry. My dad, he's a younger guy, not your husband. You got it all mixed up."

"What kind of man would abandon such a beautiful girl?" she asked.

"That's what I'm trying to find out."

"I'd never live with a man ever again," she said. "Can't trust them. Never could. Never will. You shouldn't either." She wagged her finger at me.

I started backing down the stairs.

"You all alone?" she asked.

"My friend is waiting for me in the car."

"You be careful," she warned. "There's a lot of trouble running around out there."

The door slammed shut, and I heard a series of metal locks click one after another, then the porch light went out. I stood there for a second looking up at the second-floor window, then slowly backed down the steps. The wind went out of my breath and I felt myself suffocating, as if I had suddenly stopped breathing and had no idea how to start. I sat on the steps and tried to regain my composure.

It was gone. It was just a wish. Nothing changed. I walked back over to Tracy's car, opened the door and climbed inside.

"What happened?" Tracy asked.

"Wrong house. He moved. I don't know." I stared out the window, swelling with disappointment. Once again Dad had somehow slipped from my grasp. All I wanted to know was that he was okay, whether he thought I was too, whether he was a good man or a bad man, whether he's making it or still trying. I feel like I'm stuck in a never-ending breakup. He's there even when he's not there. Dad the friendly ghost.

THE DOGS

ALL night long I dreamt of my father. Tossing and turning, he popped in and out of my conscience with the agility of an acrobat. At one point he looked like my mechanic and then Bobby was my dad and we met in the park and went on a boat to a famous landmark, but I can't remember which one, then all of a sudden he fell overboard and I awoke in a panic.

Mom was screaming at the top of her lungs. It was horrible, an incredible bloodcurdling shrill you only hear in the best B movies. She was freaking overtime. I jumped out of my bed and ran downstairs.

"What happened?" I asked. "Whatsa matter?"

Mom pointed toward the front door, then went and called the authorities. I went to the window and that's when I saw it. Sometime during the night our driveway had been sprinkled with dog corpses. There was a German shepherd with its neck twisted sideways and two mutts that were shot and dumped on our doorstep. Strewn one beside another, flies hovered over their cold bodies. A horrible stench hung in the air. In the center of it all was a DieHard battery.

The police arrived on the scene *el pronto* and questioned us all to death. They asked my mom if she was a witch and whether she ever practiced animal sacrifice or any other satanic rituals, then they wanted to know if she had any underworld connections, did she owe anybody money, were there narcotics hidden on the premises? A few neighbors stood on the edge of their lawns, pointing, looking curious, but keeping their distance. Our house had been marked by the devil himself, some children of Manson had visited, left their gifts, and departed, sparing the intended victims of death but haunting the house forever.

A yellow Department of Contagious Diseases truck rolled up and parked beside the mailbox. A couple of guys wearing white masks and rubber gloves jumped out and cautiously approached the animals. They leaned over each dog and shined a flashlight into their ears and mouth, as if maybe they'd all been attacked by fleas or plague. Then they took out some other equipment and did air samples, as if the house might be leaking radiation or something.

My mom thought it was some sort of tasteless gesture by a jealous one-night stand and gave the police a greatest hits list of her latest conquests, but I knew the dogs were intended for me. The locker fire was just the beginning. Somehow I got hooked up with Mr. Way-Wrong Loser and now the playground was haunted. I gave Mom another Valium, and when the hysteria finally settled down a bit I called Tracy.

"I hope they fucking got cholera!" she screamed. Tracy acted all tough at first, but I could tell her bravado was getting a little less intense. Her kamikaze spirit had been deflated slightly in the last twenty-four hours. She wasn't her usual Rambo self.

"First my locker, now this. I don't like it."

"It's just mind games," she said.

"Well, they work." I was beyond panic.

"Listen, in a few days we'll graduate and all this will just be an extra notch in your bedpost."

"I don't have any notches in my bedpost, thank you." I shifted the phone to my other ear. "The cops were here again. They asked about the car battery."

"What did you tell them?" she asked.

"I told them we didn't have a car."

"Did they say anything about Bobby?"

"No. Why doesn't he call me?"

"He seems to have a lot on his plate right now."

"So do I!"

"Well at least you two have something in common."

"What are we going to do?"

"What can we do?"

"Well, I'm not just going to sit around and wait to be killed by a bunch of beer guzzling dog murderers. They know where I live! I think I should come clean with the cops. It's the only way out of this."

"Are you crazy? That's exactly what Neckbrace wants you to do. You'll go to jail!"

I was getting so paranoid I started to wonder if I could even trust Tracy. If I was the curse, wouldn't that benefit her? Wouldn't she go on to live a long life full of hundreds of boyfriends? This whole thing was getting too far out of hand. "I have to go. I'll talk to you later."

I found a cigarette in Mom's purse, then went out on the porch to watch the last carcass get stuffed into a white plastic bag and dragged away. I started smoking in junior high because I thought it made me look older; when I got older I said to myself that it made me more introspective. Now it's just a stinky habit that ignites fierce retribution in the morning.

I flicked the half-burned cigarette into the yard, then got the hose out of the garage and washed down the driveway. The neighbors were still hovering together in bathrobes, staring. Even Jewels was up bright and early for the excitement, pretending to retrieve his mail for a closer look.

I felt incredibly nauseated, my stomach was a brewing sludge pit of indigestion, so I turned off the hose and went and sat on the toilet for a while. A pair of dark purple loops hung under my eyes. My hands trembled slightly. My gums were sore. My head was throbbing. I finished my business, splashed some water on my face, brushed my teeth, then went downstairs to make coffee and slam some Advil. My brother was in the kitchen sprinkling sugar over his Froot Loops.

"I had a dream about you last night." He twisted his head back and forth, as if to jar loose the memory. "It was real creepy," he said. "You want to hear it?"

"No," I said, but then changed my mind. I was anxious for anyone's vision of the future.

"You ran in front of an early morning freight train and got splattered into smithereens. I woke up right after that one." He poured milk over his cereal.

"That's it?" I asked.

"Weird, huh?" He shrugged his shoulders.

HELP

WHEN the floodwater finally receded it left a foot-wide ring around David's basement bedroom. Mom and I helped bleach the walls and scrub the floor, but it still reeked big-time. Every table and chair had to be wiped down. My brother and his friend Dylan had moved all the good stuff upstairs as the water crested, but there were still a few bits and pieces of David's past scattered in the wake: a guitar pick, an old baseball card, some girl's earring, and a few misplaced CDs.

"So what are you going to do when I leave?" Mom asked.

"What do you mean?" my brother replied.

"Well, I mean, if I move in with Dan?"

David sat on that one. I was trying to read between the lines as fast as I could. It was so out of character for Mom. It was as if they were—breaking up.

"I don't know," he said. "I guess I never thought about it."

As much as his answer sounded lame to me I really didn't have a better one. I guess I always assumed I would follow Mom, but now she seemed to be letting us know that the band might break up. It was a warning flare.

The phone started ringing, so I hurried upstairs.

"Hello?"

"Is Chrissie there?"

I was shocked. It was the boy wonder, man with a plan, Jesus of Joliet, my constant distraction.

"Where have you been?" I asked.

"I need your help," he said.

"What kind of help?" I asked.

"I need to borrow some money."

"You think I have money?"

"I don't need a lot," he said. "I'll pay you back. I swear."

Bobby was talking fast. He sounded like he had run to the phone booth or wherever the hell it was he was calling from.

"What's the emergency?"

"The cops. They raided the garage. They took the car, the tools, everything! It's all gone!"

"What happened?"

"Fucking cops. Fuck if I know. I have to get out of here . . ." He paused and I could hear him breathing. "You gotta lend me some money."

"What about that vampire babe—Ashtray Influenza or whatever the hell her name is? I'm sure she's got a bottomless cash register."

"The cops shut down the bar. It's like some big conspiracy or something."

I picked up the phone and dragged it into my room. I felt

guilty I hadn't warned him, but it wasn't like I didn't try. The panic in his voice frightened me.

"You ever been to the Empress?" he asked.

"The casino?" I walked over and sat down on the edge of my bed. "So, are you a card shark too?" I asked him.

"I need to put together some money—fast." He sounded desperate.

"The Empress seems more like a place to lose a lot of money fast," I said.

"I'm running out of choices," he said.

"What about making money the old-fashioned way?" I asked.

"I don't have time for that!"

"But you have time to pick up strangers' cars and tow them down to Joliet?"

"You don't know that happened and you better stop believing it."

"I know your priorities, Bobby, and that's enough for me to slap together a few puzzle pieces. You've got motive and there are people looking for you."

"And that's why I've got to get the hell out of here!" he shouted into the phone. "Are you going to help me or what?"

"I'll lend you some money, but I don't want you to blow it in fifteen minutes."

"I'm not gonna blow it. I know what I'm doing," he said. "You only get ahead by taking chances."

"Yeah, but with you, the stakes get a little higher each day, don't they?"

"Listen, I don't have time to play fucking games."

Bobby was freaking out. I felt sorry for him. There was no

changing Bobby. His idea of life was to keep accelerating, with the hope that he'll be able to turn the wheel in the nick of time.

"Please lend me some money. It'll be all right. I promise," he said.

"Okay. Okay. Okay. I'll get you some money. But only if I can come along."

"I'll be there in half an hour."

CASINO

GAMBLING is like an expressway to your destiny. To try and win at cards was like betting on chaos. We were riding toward the end of the movie, that was my gut feeling. It didn't seem right, it didn't have any natural qualities, it was so out of the blue and random. To me, Bobby seemed like a person moving backward, as if time were running away from him. His voice was heavy, and I could tell he hadn't been eating. He looked thin and distraught. His mind was somewhere else. He didn't say anything, although he seemed to be having continuous rambling monologues with himself.

Watching the promises of billboards along the highway I was stirring over the idea that this mission smelled of doom and I was the good-luck charm. The car roared down the express lane. My mechanic gnawed a toothpick, a strange smirk leaking from the corner of his mouth. He reached over and touched my knee, pulled it toward him, slid his hand between my thighs and up under my dress. I closed my eyes and lay back on the headrest.

"Nobody gets rich standing still," he said. And I just wondered if that were true.

I opened my eyes as we rolled up the exit ramp. Joliet was the end of nowhere. Most of the storefronts were boarded up. Gangs had staked turf. The only new industry was the casino. A woman was shot in the parking lot a few weeks after it opened. Some people called it a tragedy, others said it was a baptism.

The parking lot was jammed. Bobby found a spot in the back under a light pole marked KING TUT. We got out of the car and marched toward the front door. The casino was actually a barge floating in the canal. Gambling is only legal in the water. The barge was camouflaged with decor as ostentatious and permanent as a Fourth of July float. Egyptian-style sphinxes guarded the entrance, plastic chandeliers hung over industrial carpeting. A few green plants filled the corners. Bobby kept his hand planted firmly around my waist. I liked it, but he seemed unusually needy, which made me nervous. He sliced through the crowd, pulling me by the hand. We were like a snaking train of hope racing through a room of chaos.

People stared at the slot machines like they were deep in a trance, cranking the handles, waiting for a crash of coins to come spilling into their tin trays; others sat stonefaced at the blackjack tables, holding their cards close to the green velvet. Winning. Losing. It was very hard to concentrate. Bells were ringing, people were shouting, everything was designed to be as loud as possible.

"What an incredible collection of freaks," Bobby said, leaning against the bar. "Where do they all come from?"

"From here," I said. "Same place as me."

My mechanic bellyed up to a $100 blackjack table. The dealer looked like the mother of two, maybe three, and had the steadiness of a bartender at 3 A.M. in the face of all-night drinkers. Bobby placed his chips on the table and the cards were dispensed from the automatic shuffler. I looked across the room and saw the same nervous face at every table. The casino seemed to hold the mixed euphoria of a wedding and a funeral in the same room. The first hand had all the nervous anticipation of a first dance. My mechanic kept his cards, the dealer took one and busted. Bobby won with a seventeen, and I must say I was relieved. He was up right away and even kissed me on the cheek while waiting for the new cards.

Bobby carefully lifted his cards one at a time, and I could tell the dealer was checking out his body language to get a clue as to what he was holding. Bobby never looked at me or at the dealer. He kept his eyes on the cards.

"I'll hold," Bobby said. The dealer took two and busted again.

When the chips crossed over to Bobby I could see his eyes light up and his heart ignite with a feverish gleam of glossy destiny. It was scary really. I realized he was a person willing to gamble his last dime on the slender chance that he might win five more.

Bobby won two in a row, but when the dealer took the next three and all the chips passed back to the house, I felt as if a hole had just been drilled through my heart where all the hope used to be stored. He never won on the racetrack, so why would he win here? Bobby was down to his last bet, and he suddenly looked like someone who had just licked the envelope of doom. I wanted him to win, but deep inside I wanted him to lose too, if only in a selfish bid to keep him from running away.

Bobby looked at his cards with the same facelessness of the times before, only this time he seemed to be curling closer to the table, as if he were wilting. He took one card and busted. Bobby lost and the little money he had was gone. The dealer scooped up his last chips, then picked up the cards. Bobby stared silently for a moment, as if he were trying to control whatever was bubbling up inside. He looked shattered, as if he'd just swallowed what was left of his pride. Bobby took me by the hand and led me through the crowd. He was very upset, but I didn't feel very sorry for him.

Bobby was always looking for shortcuts in life, whether stealing a car to race the next weekend, or throwing money at a blackjack table to fund an evacuation. He was trying to walk on water and the waves kept sweeping over his head. But even in his worst element, I still felt incredibly attracted to him. Part of me was watching somebody walk a tightrope without a net, and part of me was wishing I were brave enough to walk too. It was a double-edged butter knife knowing my life was exciting because it was attached to his.

When we got out to the car I tried to swing his mood in another direction, but he was sullen as a tree.

"I'm so fucking stupid," he said.

"Listen, just because it didn't happen this time doesn't mean it won't happen next time."

"It ain't never gonna happen."

"Don't say that."

"Why not?"

"Because pretty soon you'll start believing it," I said.

Even though Bobby was the kind of person whose setbacks only gave him more determination, for me, it was as if the balloon had popped and the party was almost over. I didn't see any light at the end of the tunnel. I put my arm around his waist and hugged him. And then he leaned down and kissed me in the middle of the parking lot. And these kisses were a whole lot different from the ones the night we watched the fire. It was as if he meant it.

"You believe in me, don't you?" he asked with surprise in his voice, as if I was the first person who ever did.

"You're the kind of person who chases destiny instead of letting destiny chase you," I said. "There's a lot of bumps on that road."

Bobby seemed incredibly vulnerable. He clung to me like I was going to save him. He kissed me again, but this time the kisses felt distant again, as if he were already thinking about his next plan. I kissed him as if to lure him back from wherever he was headed.

"C'mon," he said. "Let's go."

THE TRAILER

BOBBY took me to his trailer. It was perched in a sliver of woods, a hedge of tangled shrubbery and weeds bordering the far side of an unfinished development overlooking Bolingbrook Mall. The mall failed ten or twenty years ago and was still boarded up. The weathered plywood was coated with fresh graffiti. The plastic sign along the road had been punched out by gunfire.

The mall once housed an indoor amusement park with a roller coaster, merry-go-round, and even a Ferris wheel. Clowns gave away free balloons, carnival music was piped in from the ceiling. What was billed as a shopping Disneyland turned out to be a pathetic attempt to give local carnies a year-round venue. Cheap hot dog shacks opened side by side with little flea market–type knickknack tables. It looked like a rummage sale with three-hundred-foot ceilings. It was always ghost city.

Bobby's trailer was surrounded by waist-high weeds, stacks of tires, and empty beer cans. Leaning against the rusty shed were souvenirs from his job: bumpers, fenders, and hubcaps galore. It looked like it may have once been painted swimming pool green, but that was a long time ago.

When we got out of the car I could hear the power lines sizzling overhead: snap, crackle, pop. The wind tore through the bushes and howled around the trailer. Bobby's wind chimes rang a constant alarm. Scanning the perimeter I kept thinking I saw something moving just beyond the corner of my eye.

"Your place sure is spooky," I said.

"Keeps the ghosts away," he replied.

Bobby popped the door open, and I slipped into the mouth of the trailer. The smell hit me first, then Bobby turned on the light and I looked around in awe. Bobby's trailer was a pigsty. There was garbage scattered all over the place. A small sunken brown couch covered with crushed Styrofoam cups and grease-stained paper plates faced a portable television resting on a milk crate. Red wax had melted over the armrests of the couch, the Big Gulp cups on both sides were filled with cigarette butts. The sink was piled with crusty dishes. The carpeting had probably never seen a vacuum cleaner, and there were fruit flies buzzing around everywhere.

"Sorry about the mess." He cleared a spot on the couch for me. "The maid is on vacation."

"You have a maid?" I asked. "How fancy." I pulled a picture of Asha Lorenza off the refrigerator. "Is this her?" I held it up to him.

"No." He laughed. "You want to watch TV or something?"

Bobby rescued two Budweisers from the refrigerator, cracked them open, and handed me one. I dropped Asha's picture behind the couch, then dialed in a Godzilla movie just in time for some awesome Tokyo destruction. Bobby plopped down next to me and put his arm around my shoulder. I curled under his arm and traced the muscles of his smooth stomach.

I could tell he was still upset. Bobby's eyes were dilated and he had that unreadable look, trapped in that spacey boy thing, a million thoughts circling the wagon train.

"Quarter for your thoughts," I said.

"Big spender." He seemed impressed.

"You're worth it."

"I was just imagining flying to the moon."

"How come you're always dreaming about someplace else?"

"I like to project myself out of this trailer. I don't need to explain that, do I?"

"At least you have a trailer," I said. I looked at his face, his hair, trying to read the lines stretching from the corners of his eyes. His whole face looked like history. I was trying to decide whether it had a future. He seemed like a white-trash miracle, one of those boys from a long line of rednecks who pops out of nowhere and takes over the world. I was certain Bobby was more than he even knew.

"So where you gonna go?" I asked.

"North Carolina maybe. I got some cousins down there," he said between sips of beer. "You oughta come with me."

"What?"

"You'd like it. There's lots of trees and hills and the air smells good, not like around here."

Bobby's idea came so far out of the blue I wasn't quite sure how to digest it. I couldn't tell if he meant what he was saying or was just talking off his sleeve.

"You mean it?" I asked.

"Why not?" he asked. "I need a good-luck charm."

My heart swung on a pendulum. I wanted to, but I had to think about it. He equated me with a trinket on a bracelet, and that's a long throw from unconditional love. Mom did announce that from here on out it was every person for themselves, only I wasn't sure I wanted to check into the first motel on the list. Not that I could afford it anyway. Plus, Bobby was a mystery wrapped around an enigma, who knows where that plane was going to land. He could tell by my silence that I was standing on the fence.

"You gotta bust out of your cocoon sooner or later," he said.

"I haven't even graduated yet!" I laid on his bed with a smile of possibility racing through my nervous system, but at the same time a streak of sadness was eating at my heart. I wasn't sure I could bare for him to leave now, but I was even less secure with the idea of being his companion. He leaned over and kissed me and held me so tight I had a feeling that maybe this was destiny dropping its hook in my stream and it was up to me whether or not to take the bait.

My heart was racing with love and worry. I imagined visiting Bobby in the hospital, visiting him in jail, but never in the winner's circle. I looked over at my mechanic and watched him breathe in the milky morning light. Outside I could hear cars on the highway hurling into the distance. Inside everything was perfectly still, only a patchwork of stale smells competed for my attention. The fold-out couch was so small there was nowhere to move. I closed my eyes and let my thoughts parade around in circles. The Godzilla movie ended, and the television became a snow pattern of fuzzy blue light warming the room like an electric fireplace.

"Bobby?" I whispered. "I have to go home."

He rolled over and kissed me, then slid his hand up my shirt.

"Now?" he asked.

"Well, not this second."

FIRECRACKER

THE sun came up and started to bake the trailer. I woke up sweating. I sat at the edge of the couch and found myself trying to snap together a few buttons between when I left home and where I was now. Bobby was anxious and flopped around the trailer like a fish out of water. When he finally burst outside all the warmth of the couch was replaced with the creeping chill of dawn, all the romance of the night before was exchanged for the complications of sunlight.

I walked out to the car and Bobby whisked me home. The sky was lit by an overlapping pattern of mushy gray clouds. The car felt cold and had a hollowness to it that I had never noticed before. All I wanted to do was brush my teeth and curl up in my bed, but then I realized I might have to deal with Mom. Hopefully she spent the night with the astronaut. Bobby looked tired and worried and anxious to get me out of the car.

When we pulled up in front of my house I planted a major kiss on his face.

"I have to try and get a hold of Danny," he said, checking his rearview mirror, as if we might have been followed. "He might be able to help me out."

"I wish there was something I could do," I said.

"I'll be all right." He tried to be reassuring.

"I can probably scrape together another hundred dollars," I said.

"I feel so lame taking your money, especially after what happened." He seemed embarrassed.

"You're not taking it. You're borrowing it. I know you need it and I know you're the type to return a favor. Maybe I'm a fool, but I like the idea of you owing me something."

"I gotta leave tonight," he said. "Should we meet somewhere?"

"I'll have to go downtown to get the money. How about Starbuck's or the Tivoli Lanes? I don't think anything else is open."

"Let's do the bowling alley." He checked his mirror again. "What time?"

"Sometime after eight," I said.

He leaned over and kissed me, then shifted the car into gear. I knew it was time for me to disappear. I didn't know what to say. And even though he asked me to come with him, there was an overwhelming feeling in my heart that I might never see him again. He had a look on his face that was anything but reassuring.

"Be careful, Bobby." I got out of the car and closed the door, then watched him bank around the cul-de-sac corner and accelerate up the hill. My heart sank into my stomach. There's nothing worse than falling in love with impossibility. I picked up the newspaper and headed up the driveway.

There was a strange beeping sound coming from the side of the house. I walked around to check it out, and there was Grandma scanning the yard for treasure or something. She was wearing headphones and waving a broom-size electric wand over the grass. When she saw me she waved me over.

"What are you doing, Grandma?" I asked.

"Oh, just snooping." She pulled her headphones off. "The microphones on this baby are so powerful I can hear the earthworms eating breakfast."

"That's lovely," I said.

"You're up awfully early," Grandma said. "I usually never see anything stirring around here until way past nine."

"I was just getting the paper."

"Was that the paperboy?" she asked.

"Who? That?" I scrambled to reshuffle my story. "That was Bobby. The guy I was telling you about."

"You look a little shook up. What's the matter?"

I didn't answer her and she knew I was hiding something.

"If you can't trust me you can't trust anybody," she said. "And that's a terrible place to be." She shook her head and looked down at the grass.

"I trust you, Grandma, it's just hard for me to talk about."

Grandma turned off her gadget. "Some men are like holding a firecracker in your hand," she said. "They're exciting when the fuse is lit, but if you hold on too long the results can be real painful."

"You can say that again."

"Sometimes you gotta throw it and get out of the way."
She jumped a step to animate her idea. "It's gonna hurt, but
not as much as if you try to hold on."

Grandma slipped on her headphones and went back to her
lost treasure. I wasn't sure I agreed or even wanted to agree
with all of Grandma's prophecies, but I walked up behind her
and gave her a huge hug anyway.

"I love you, Grandma," I said.

"I love you too, Chrissie." Grandma disappeared behind an
evergreen.

I gave a short prayer to the God of missing moms and slid
my key into the slot, pushed the door open, and quickly unlaced my shoes. The house was dead silent. I crept into the
kitchen, found the note from Mom, and felt a major sense of
relief. There was a reference to money, but I'm sure that was
long gone into the bloodstream of my brother. I took a banana
out of the fruit bowl, then climbed the stairs and fell onto my
bed. I tried to focus on some schoolwork because I've got so
many reports due now it's not funny. For English, I'm finishing
an essay on slacker god Winnie-the-Pooh; for science, I'm taking on space junk, which basically has no real function other
than to make the weather more exciting on the six o'clock
news; and for history, I'm photographing the hundred and fifty
Sears-Roebuck homes built in Downers Grove. I've only done
one roll of film, so it's gonna be hell around here for a while.
Are you there, God? It's me, Chrissie.

The trouble with love is that it's never perfect. When it
comes to mating the fit has to be tight as two puzzle pieces,
any space between personalities only gets bigger. The space in
between Mom and Dad was like a truck stop, a place to say

hello and order pancakes. Bobby is supercharged trouble. I can deal with his messy trailer, but I wasn't sure I wanted to be the Bonnie for his Clyde. Our relationship felt similar to riding an escalator that keeps returning to the same floor, I knew I was never going any higher on the priority list.

I closed my eyes and raced toward a whiteness so pure it was colorless, but all my thoughts circled back to the mechanic, his car, his trailer, his garage, his incredibly romantic and disasterous life. The vagabond car thief probably has a carbon copy past of his more than reckless present. He drifted here without directions and would probably disappear with the same abandon. One of these days he's going to make the wrong turn and end up trapped by his own ambition. I just hope he survives the transition.

TIVOLI LANES

TRACY was stressing over finals, the curse, and her lack of a serious relationship this close to summer and the last thing she wanted to do was go knock down some pins at Tivoli Lanes. I called her anyway.

"Hello?" Tracy said.

"Remember all the favors I've done for you lately?" I asked.

"No."

"Like introducing you to that guy at the garage?"

"I introduced myself and he never called me. Get to the point."

"I need a humongous favor. Please, please, please come to the bowling alley with me for an hour."

"Tracy lets go here. Tracy lets go there. I am not your chauffeur. Besides, my mom is using the car."

"Then we'll have to walk."

"Oh yeah, right. Walk. I'm sure."

"It's the last chance I'll ever get to see him! Tracy—I'll owe you forever."

"You already owe me forever."

"Listen, I'll talk to my brother."

"I've heard that promise before."

"Please! I'm begging!"

"Are you on your knees?"

"Tracy, please!"

There was a long silence, but finally Tracy gave in. "All right. I'll be over in a little while."

Tracy was late as usual. "I can't believe we're walking," she said. It was only about a fifteen-minute walk downtown, but Tracy made sure it seemed like days. We stopped at the bank and I withdrew another hundred dollars.

"You shouldn't give him any more money," Tracy said. I knew it was wrong, but I also knew that Tracy would have done the exact same thing if she were in my shoes.

The bowling alley was tucked underground opposite the Main Street train station. It still smelled like the fifties, a sweet mix of Brylcreem, soda pop, and cigarettes. The air-conditioning was on year-round so you always had to bring a sweater. The old-timer behind the bar looked like he'd been there since the day they opened. He was watching the Sox game, blasting from the color TV perched over the bar like an electronic gargoyle. We ordered root beers and spiked them with miniatures. Vodka and root beer was my favorite. The old man handed us our shoes—a pair of fives and a pair of sixes—then I went and found my favorite purple sparkle ball. Tracy always goes first.

Tracy got up and cooled her hand over the air vent, then

retrieved her ball and let it rip. She had a very quick release, as if her ball was just one more burden she couldn't wait to get rid of. I sat at the scorer's table and filled in all the preliminary information.

Needless to say I bowled like shit. Tracy on the other hand was on a roll. The gutterball queen even had a strike. Bobby didn't show up until the sixth frame. He slipped in unnoticed and dropped into an orange Formica chair.

"You got a cigarette?" he asked. I handed him one of Tracy's. He looked paranoid and untrustworthy, but still had an air of innocence clinging to him that made him completely adorable, like a dog who ate all the cake and was left outside the screen door.

"You mad at me or something?" he asked.

"Why should I be mad? You disappear, you reappear. You're like a superhero to me."

"I don't make the rules."

"You don't follow them either."

Tracy beat me for the very first time. I couldn't concentrate. I was trying to figure out a way to keep Bobby from running away. I could get in the car and go for a ride, but in the back of my mind I knew that if he got caught there would be something in it for me too, and who knows how much farther he would be willing to go when things got truly desperate. Bobby reeked of hard time, and I knew in my heart that he wasn't the type to surrender. When the police came to his window it would not be pretty.

I unlaced my shoes and slipped into my romper stompers.

"Imagine if AIDS was a foot disease," Tracy said.

"The entire Midwest would have been devestated," I said.

"What are you two talking about?" Bobby asked.

"Girl talk," I said.

I set my bowling shoes on the counter and led Bobby up the steep stairs. A train was rolling through town and it had the sound of destiny wrapped all around it. Bobby looked anxious and I knew he wanted to go. I knew there was nothing I could do to stop him. I kissed him in front of the Tivoli Hotel like I never wanted him to forget me. He rubbed his hand in my hair, then down my back. I laid my head on his chest and listened to the train wheels clack and squeal. Bobby smelled like smoke and nervous sweat. I started leaning away from him, but he just clung tighter.

"You're not going, are you?" He sounded remorseful. I looked into Bobby's eyes and suddenly realized how lonely he truly was, that he really had no one to turn to, that he more than likely had nowhere to go, that everything he told me about his past was probably lies or pleasant landscapes he'd created for himself. Why else would he be so aloof and yet so needy?

He waited for an answer.

"I can't," I said.

Bobby looked both ways, as if the cops were ready to ambush us any second. I reached in my pocket and handed him another portion of my life savings. He took it and stuffed it in his pocket.

"It's not much," I said.

"It's more than I deserve." He leaned over and kissed me. "I really appreciate it." He looked up as the last cars of the train whizzed by, smiling nervously, trying to be reassuring, but Bobby was obviously completely unsure himself. He shook

his car keys, as if he got what he came for and was now anxious
to get the show on the road. "I wish there was some way I
could return the favor," he said.

"How about a ride home," Tracy said before I could say
anything.

Bobby led us around the back of the Tivoli Theater to an
alley garage. Tracy took the backseat and I sat up front with
my mechanic. Bobby cranked the stereo. It was too loud to
talk, so I just leaned against the car door and watched Bobby
drive. Tracy and I occasionally glanced at each other, but that
was the extent of our communication. Bobby was wired,
smoking like a fiend. His lips moved slowly, as if he were
having some kind of private confession with the voices in his
head. Oncoming headlights flushed the car with pockets of
light, black shadows slid through the car.

When we pulled up to the intersection at Fifty-fifth and Main
I glanced out the window and watched my worst nightmare roll
up beside us. I saw them and they saw me. Neckbrace and his
friends jumped out of the car and started barking like dogs.

"What's this all about?" my mechanic asked.

"Go!" I said.

My mechanic looked at me like I was crazy. "It's a red
light." He pointed.

"Go!"

"I see they got a new windshield." Tracy laughed.

"It's a different car," I said.

The monsters circled Bobby's car. Neckbrace took a swing
with a baseball bat and knocked out a front headlight.

"Who the fuck are these assholes?" Bobby threw his car in
reverse and nearly backed over the onion-headed one.

"Jealous boyfriends," Tracy said.

Bobby made a U-turn in reverse and took off down Main Street. Chuckie and his collection of future ex-convicts piled back into their car and gave chase. My mechanic turned left onto Maple, but the deathcar was right behind us. He turned right into Denburn Woods, but they stuck with us like paint.

I was waiting for some smart-aleck comment from the backseat, but Tracy was busy trying to figure out how the seat belt worked.

"Why are these guys so angry with you?" my mechanic asked.

"Wormface tried to rape the dish of Downers Grove," Tracy shouted while looking out the back window. "We gave them a little medicine, but I guess they need another dose."

"What did she say?"

"The last time they fucked with us one of them ended up in the hospital." I turned and saw the deathcar racing up behind us.

"Chrissie threw a car battery through their windshield," Tracy yelled.

He looked over at me and smiled. "That wasn't very nice," he said.

"Hey, wait five minutes, you'll want to throw a battery through their windshield too," I protested.

Bobby swerved through one cul-de-sac after another, winding back toward the tracks. This was the first time I ever prayed for cops. There are eight zillion cops in Downers Grove and not one anywhere in sight. They were probably all busy busting a kegger in Woodridge or something.

The deathcar stayed on our case, skipping stop signs. When we got trapped at a traffic light the white plague pulled up beside us and began hooting and hollering like a bunch of dogs again. My valentine waved a gun at us while his buddy in the backseat made obscene gestures with a baseball bat.

"Oh my God, he's got a gun." I shook Bobby's arm.

"What an asshole," Tracy said. "Thinks he's a fucking Quentin Tarantino or something."

"I don't need this right now," Bobby chipped in.

When the light turned green Bobby accelerated and the deathcar followed beside us. Neckbrace reached out of the window and fired his gun at Bobby's front tire.

"Oh my God, he shot at us." I grabbed Bobby's arm.

"Let go!" He shook away my hand. Bobby swerved onto the shoulder and almost took out a mailbox. He looked worried and that made me even more scared.

"We need to find some cops," Tracy shouted. "That guy is fucking crazy. He'll kill us." Bobby pulled ahead and cut them off. Neckbrace and his friends swerved into the right lane and rolled up beside us.

"No cops," Bobby said. "Ask him if he wants to race."

"What?"

"Go ahead, ask him."

"Are you crazy?" I asked.

"My car against his, winner takes all."

Tracy rolled down her window and tilted her head toward them.

"You're dead, bitch!" my sweetheart said, pointing his gun at her. "You and the other one. We don't care about the faggot." He laughed, as if what he said was funny.

"My friend wants to race his car against yours, what do you say?" Tracy asked.

"You want to race?" He seemed surprised, then turned to his friends. They discussed it for about half a second, then my valentine pointed his gun right at me. I about shit in my pants.

"We're just gonna wait until you run out of gas." He laughed hysterically like some psycho wanna-be, then turned and took another shot at Bobby's front tire. Missed again. Bobby accelerated and pulled ahead of them.

"Fasten your seat belts," he said.

"They already are," Tracy said.

Both cars rolled side by side with increasing speed. The next light seemed as distant as an airplane in the sky. The two cars accelerated at a wreckless pace, dipping into the first hill and rising up the next.

"Get down." My mechanic pressed my head beside him. "Cover your face." I grabbed the seat belt and braced my feet under the glove compartment. Bobby swerved out into the opposite lane like he had lost control, but then whipped the car back and punched the front end of the deathcar. My legs banged against the door. Bobby slammed on the brakes and the car spun around in a half-circle, then came to a stop. I leaped up and saw the deathcar jump the curb and veer into someone's front yard. It seemed to swerve slightly to avoid the house, but then slammed into a massive oak tree. There was a huge explosion of shattered glass as the car wrapped around the tree, flipped over, and rolled into the other end of the house, finally coming to rest upside down in the next driveway.

"Oh my God." Tracy crawled up from the backseat.

"Are you all right?" Bobby asked.

We both nodded. I was speechless. I cut a quick glance across the yard but couldn't really see anything. A house light went on and then the porch light. My mechanic turned off onto a side street and drove steadily away from the accident.

"I hope he's happy with himself," Bobby said.

"Thrilled, I'm sure," Tracy responded.

GRADUATION DAY

MOM sat in the grandstand with Grandma and my brother, snapping pictures with her Instamatic camera to glue into the family scrapbook, proof this really happened.

I wore a white dress under my blue graduation gown and threw my flat cap into the sky like everyone else, but that's where the similarity ended.

ALCOHOL BLAMED IN THE DEATH OF THREE TEENS, the headline said.

"It's so perfect," Tracy whispered. "The world will never know." Her slippery kitty-cat face smiled ear to ear. "And who could have known that Skyler Dickerson was on board?"

It turns out Skyler was some minor football guy who ended up in the wrong posse at the wrong time. He was my age. He was in my class. Nobody else will ever know him, but nobody in my class will ever forget him.

I was relieved the curse had been fulfilled, but I wish I hadn't witnessed it from the front row. It could have just as easily been me. Whenever I close my eyes I see flashbacks of my valentine and then the crash. I still feel trapped in the moment. I never liked him, but I never wanted to see him die.

"They always seemed a little shifty to me," I heard one teacher say to another, "but almost all the kids give me the creeps these days."

Most of my classmates were stunned. Parents hovered close to their children. Everyone seemed overwhelmed by the collision of grief and joy. An eerie quiet descended over the football field when the principal bowed his head and asked for a moment of silent prayer. Speeches floated by like painted wind. I couldn't hear any of it, my ears were still buzzing with accusations from the corners of my guilty conscience.

Tracy said not to worry, that the story would fade as quickly as soap bubbles in the bathtub, but when the memorials and testimonials began about the "three promising young men" I felt an overwhelming compulsion to run up to the microphone and confess everything. Some girls were crying, some were holding flowers. It was very upsetting to think people my own age were dead. I could feel sweat gathering in every pore of my body. The ceremony seemed to go on forever and ever. Nobody really stuck their neck out for them, besides some cheerleader who recited a cheeseball poem about them waiting for her in the sky. Some kid down the row started cracking up and then a few others did too, and that made me feel a little better. I felt sorry for Neckbrace and his hooligans, but life spills, and it's every marble for itself. When those two cars kissed, my heart just about exploded with terror. I thought for sure I was gonna pull a Princess Di.

"You know we're going to hell for this," I told Tracy as we marched out of the football field.

"We have time to make up for it." Tracy took off her sunglasses, cleaned them with the sleeve of her graduation gown. "Think of it this way. It was a test. We passed." She put her glasses back on. "I have to go deal with my grandparents. Call me later."

I stumbled around the tipped-over folding chairs cluttering the football field and wound passed the crowd clogging the entrance to the parking lot, scanning my peripheral vision for guys with sunglasses and walkie-talkies, still certain that the county sheriff would be waiting with a paddy wagon, that handcuffs would be strapped to my wrists any moment now. I looked over at the school, then back across the football field. A queasy wisp of nostalgia tidal waved through my jaded system.

That's when I saw my mom's old Ford at the far end of the lot and my mechanic standing beside it. I felt a lump in my throat, ran over, and kissed him a good one.

"What are you doing here?" I asked. "I expected you to be long gone by now." I glanced around the parking lot, more paranoid than ever. Bobby looked as if he hadn't slept all night. He was gaunt and shaky, sucking a cigarette as if it were his only source of nutrition.

"Wouldn't want to miss the big day," he said. "Did they give you your piece of paper?" he asked.

"Got it." I waved it up in the air. "Where did you get my mom's car? I thought it was a goner."

"The guys at the station gave it to Danny. It needed a ring job, but he got it running. I had no idea it was your mom's old car, that's really bizarre." Bobby opened the door.

"It's cleaner than I've ever seen it," I said. "What happened to your car?"

"It was pretty messed up. Danny put it in deep storage. I probably should have ditched it anyway. I'm sure the cops are looking for it by now."

"So what are you doing here?"

"I just wanted to make sure you were all right," he said.

"I'm all right," I said, lifting my gown to show him the bruise on my leg.

"Nice souvenir," he said.

"Did you hear they all died?" I asked.

He nodded. "Did you know them?"

"Not really," I said.

"They didn't exactly give us a lot of room to negotiate."

"It's not your fault."

"You didn't tell anybody did you?" he asked.

"No."

Bobby seemed really freaked, and it kind of scared me to be with him now. He bounced around the car like a pinball looking for a hole.

"You sure you won't come with me?" he asked.

I couldn't say no, so I shook my head. He kissed me, as if that would change my mind, and to be honest, it almost did. I tried to be brave, but tears just fell out of my eyes and started dripping onto my graduation gown. It wasn't just Bobby. It was everything. I was so exhausted. My head swung down in self-defense.

"You gotta come," Bobby insisted.

"No, Bobby. You go if you want to. I'm staying."

"What about the cops?"

"What about them?"

"They're gonna piece the story together sooner or later."

"And so what if they do? Those fuckers shot at us. We could have been killed. They lost control of their car. It wasn't my fault. It just happened." I stared at him, but he couldn't really look at me. There were no words. Everything was transmitted through the electric silence that crackled between us. Bobby looked scared. I could see his teeth mashing side to side.

He got in the car and rolled down the window. I tried to memorize the outline of his hair, the thickness of his eyebrows, anything that would sustain the paint of memory and prevent it from peeling.

I took a deep breath. "If I get in that car I'll end up just like you," I said.

"What's wrong with that?"

"You're just gonna run away all your life, aren't you?"

"I'll stop somewhere."

"I don't see it, Bobby."

"You don't see what?"

"I don't see you stopping. I see you driving right off the edge of the world."

"Don't you want to see what the edge of the world looks like?"

I stared at him, but didn't say anything. Once again Bobby had tangled me up in my own words. He looked up at me one last time, then shifted into gear. "I'll call you when I get there." Bobby pulled away, drove up to the corner, turned right, and disappeared. I wiped away the fresh layer of tears clinging to the corner of my eye, turned, and ran across the school lawn, already regretting my decision.

THE PEAR TREES

A small brown pear tore from its sagging branch, shuttled through the leaves, and bounced on the ground like a baseball landing in centerfield. The yard was littered with saucy brown pears. Some whole, others squashed by shoes, the garden sweet with their lucious smell of decay. Hovering wasps and bees drilled into the moist nectar oozing from the rotting pears, then flew off and circled in drunken euphoria, wasted in the Garden of Eden.

I parked my blanket in the backyard, far away from everyone and everything. I wanted to be alone with my sins. I wanted a chance to breathe without feeling like someone was fighting me for the same breath.

Just like that my mechanic rolled off into the horizon. It was a horrible choice, but the two of us on the highway headed nowhere in particular was a recipe for disaster. Like a pair of dice rolling across a long green table, sooner or later we'd have to stop and deal with the consequences. And for better or worse, I wasn't ready to take those kinds of chances. I'm glad he's driving Mom's old Ford. It makes me think he'll be okay. It makes me feel like I'm still there with him, that he won't forget about me. I'm glad he got out of here without incident. I couldn't stand the thought of Bobby in jail. He was a basket of big trouble, but he did save my life.

Our relationship had the momentary intensity of a cloud-burst and I doubt I was even remotely capable of handling the potential circumstances. I already have a vagabond father, I don't need a vagabond boyfriend. I know what it's like to grow up with that big hole in your heart.

I cracked open a Diet Coke and looked up into the sky. It seemed a lot clearer since the oil fire was put to rest. The clouds were whiter than white, the sky bluer than blue. A raven on the top branch of the pear tree pushed off, swung its big black wings and sailed over the lilac bushes, high above the willow tree and beyond the power lines.

I got a call from the manager at the DQ and he said I could start as early as Monday. Hopefully I'll save up enough money to get an apartment with Tracy in the city next fall. It's going to be a whole summer of sticky red smocks, but at least there will be air-conditioning. And one thing is for sure, my social life will not suffer.

Meanwhile, my career in publishing continues to blossom. Ad revenue for the fanzine doubled and then tripled, and it looks like distribution will spread to record shops in Lombard, Hinsdale, and Lisle. People are already saying the first issue is a collector's item.

Mom's still in denial about Starman, but I have a feeling

she's just hesitant about jumping into round two without more training camp. She's still driving his car and he still pays for her dinners, so I figure she must be doing something right. I have a feeling she's just waiting for a bigger slice of pie.

David decided to keep the band together despite ominous threats from our neighbor, and I'm glad, because he finally has something to focus his attention on besides his bug zapper and gin rummy. They even got a gig at that club in Chicago, thanks to Tracy, who is now acting as their manager. If she can't have him, she's at least going to keep an eye on him. Grandma is continually locked away in her basement rewiring the forces of nature, and Dad is still absent as sunshine at midnight.

The world keeps spinning faster, and I'm still looking for a handle to hold on to, the alternatives aren't exactly a pail of cupcakes. My heart beats backward when I think of the mechanic, but I know deep in my heart that what burns today will still flicker tomorrow, and if he shows up anywhere on the map I'll find him. I'll buy the lipstick and he'll buy the beer and what happens after that is none of your business.

In the meantime, I'll be maintaining a very low profile. No sense in kicking dust in the eyes of God or anything. I'm sure She's got it out for me already.